CHASING

VICTORY

A NOVEL BY JOSHUA SHIFRIN

AN OLD LINE PUBLISHING BOOK

Printed in the United States of America

ISBN-13: 978-1-937004-27-9
ISBN-10: 1-937004-27-9

This book is a work of fiction. Any references to real people, events, establishments, organizations, or locales are intended solely to provide a sense of authenticity and are used fictitiously. All other characters, incidents, and dialogue are drawn from the author's imagination and are not to be construed as real.

Old Line Publishing, LLC
P.O. Box 624
Hampstead, MD 21074
Toll-Free Phone: 1-877-866-8820
Toll-Free Fax: 1-877-778-3756
Email: oldlinepublishing@comcast.net
Website: www.oldlinepublishingllc.com

Dedication

For Michelle – a true example of bravery and inspiration

CHAPTER 1

As Dr. Julia Pearlman addressed the sea of mournful onlookers she choked back tears and swallowed hard.

"He was the quintessential optimist," she began. "If there was ever a man who made lemonade out of lemons it was my father, Isaac Pearlman. Whether he was working at his father's shoe store in Munich at the tender age of nine or being corralled into a train to meet his certain death at Auschwitz, my father always saw an opportunity. Imagine," Julia continued, "being treated like an animal, worked literally to the bone, and still being able to open up your heart and find your soul mate. As my mother Ida, of blessed memory, used to tell my brother Michael and me on what seemed to be a daily basis, 'Who but your father could make that hellish existence not only bearable, but beautiful?'"

Under the paradoxically melancholy yet sun soaked afternoon, Julia fought to keep her composure. "Although life dealt him a tough hand, Itzy Pearlman saw it as all aces." As the mourners nodded their heads knowingly, many of them turned to gaze at Julia's brother Michael in the front row. Mikey, as he was affectionately called by all who knew him, had been born with a mild form of Down's Syndrome. But despite his disabilities he was in many ways a hero to Julia. Although Mikey lacked many of the abilities normally taken for granted he did have his father's love of life, and everyone who really knew him couldn't help but envy him to some degree.

"My father loved his friends, his community, and most of all his family, whom he often called his most cherished possession. As he often said, 'My greatest joy is to see the bond and respect my children have for one another, and to know that they will always be there for each other. For this I will be eternally grateful.' Our father was truly one of a kind. He is now reunited with his lovely bride, no doubt looking down on all of us, and once again feeling like the luckiest man to have ever lived. May God bless Itzy Pearlman, and everything that he stood for."

As Julia ended her eulogy she closed her eyes and repeated the vow that she made every day of her life - to honor her father and mother by taking care of her brother with all of the abilities that her parents and God had bestowed upon her.

CHAPTER 2

William Victory always found his name ironic. *Victory... What a joke!* he thought. For here he was again, sitting in a classroom without a clue. William was now a senior in high school, and his life had been anything but a victory. He lived with his alcoholic mother in a dilapidated, three-room apartment one story above a liquor store frequented by winos. His father had abandoned his mother "about five minutes after he found out I was pregnant, and we're better off without him," his mother repeatedly told him. "That S.O.B. was the worst thing that ever happened to me." Although William tried to convince himself otherwise, he couldn't help but think that his mother resented his father primarily for the creation of a good for nothing child - the same child that now sat in a remedial math class unable to grasp the concept of the simple algebra he should have mastered years ago.

Despite the fact that William was tall with blond hair, piercing hazel eyes, a straight nose, strong chin and angular physique, he had few friends and even fewer girls chasing him. He had somehow managed to secure a girlfriend, but with his low self-esteem William considered this to be a miracle. Even so, he couldn't care less. He was happy to be a loner. He also knew that he was a nice person. He took care of his mother seemingly seven nights a week when she would come home drunk and pass out on the sofa. He always had a kind word to say and rarely complained despite his meager circumstances. In reality, William Victory only had one complaint - he hated, *hated*, being stupid. And to make things worse, why did everyone always have to tell him to just try harder? "You're lazy, William. It's as simple as that," his no nonsense guidance counselor repeatedly told him. "You're smarter than 90% of the students in this school and yet you're barely squeaking by with D's. The world's a harsh place, William. When are you going to shape up?"

And the worst part was, William believed every word of it. The only problem was that he had been motivated. He knew from the time he was a young boy that he was playing without a safety net. With no father or siblings, and a mother who couldn't even take care of herself, William knew he was going to have to make it on his own. But after years of trying to comprehend his teachers' instructions with endless frustration, he had simply given up. *If I could just study and learn,* he thought. *If I was only half as smart as everyone has been telling me!* But William was far from smart. In reality he thought he was an idiot. He was sure of it. *Victory?* What a joke!

CHAPTER 3

Shortly after the funeral, a swarm of well-wishers filed into Julia's large, old Victorian home to perform a 'Shiva call' - a Jewish ritual in which family and friends came to give emotional support to the immediate family of the deceased. As the congregants spoke in hushed tones, they waited patiently to relay their deepest sympathies to Julia and Michael. "My dearest Julia," her Aunt Judy on her mother's side nearly whispered. "You are such an inspiration. A combined MD/PhD from Harvard, a thriving private practice, a professor at Yale and a distinguished researcher. And to take care of your older brother on top of all your other responsibilities... you have truly done your parents and your family proud."

In reality, Dr. Julia Pearlman was everything William Victory aspired to be. Sure Julia had always worked extremely hard, but things had simply come easily to her. A stellar student since kindergarten, Julia had never brought home a grade lower than an

A. And she seemed to have unending energy. She rarely slept, ate little, and took on every task, no matter how minute, as if it were a matter of national security.

"Thank you Aunt Judy, but I've far from done it on my own. With parents as encouraging and supportive as mine constantly telling me I could do anything I put my mind to, I never realized that I was doing anything out of the ordinary. I've truly been blessed," she answered modestly.

After the last of the guests finally went home, Julia and Michael sat quietly on the living room sofa, both engrossed in their own thoughts. When Michael began to cry Julia snapped back to the present. "What's the matter, Mikey?" Julia asked quietly, obviously knowing the answer.

"I miss Daddy," Michael sniffled.

"I know, honey. But Mommy and Daddy will always be there for us as long as we keep them in our hearts."

"I know," Mikey whimpered, "but I miss him anyway." As Julia slid over on the sofa to give her brother a hug she suppressed her own emotions, reminding herself to stay strong for her brother.

"I miss him too, but never forget, Mikey - I'll always be there for you. If there's ever anything you need, anything at all, you must always remember that your sister will be there for you, OK? And there's one more thing…"

"Yeah," he said as he looked at Julia expectantly.

"I love you very, very much."

A small smile penetrated Michael's lips as he answered. "I love you, too."

CHAPTER 4

As the seven days of Shiva calls came to an end, Julia needed to get back to work. In fact, she looked forward to it. Julia was never one who enjoyed idle time. The truth was that Julia was one of those lucky few who loved her work. She loved being a psychiatrist. Her parents had always stressed that making a difference in the lives of others was of the utmost importance, and Julia took this lesson to heart. After receiving a full academic scholarship to Dartmouth College and graduating with honors with a Bachelors of Science in Bio-Chemistry, medical school was the obvious choice for Julia. In reality Julia had known that she wanted to be a doctor since she won the science fair in the fifth grade, and when Harvard offered her a chance to take part in a newly formed medical degree program that combined a PhD as well she jumped at the chance, despite the extra schooling that most people would find overwhelming. After completing her first two years of medical school, it was time to start the PhD program. At this point most of the students in Julia's position had a perplexing decision to make, to say the least - which of the multitude of research options did they want to pursue? There were so many to choose from. Yet Julia, in keeping to form with her M.O., always seemed to know just what was right for her.

For her whole life Julia had felt special. Her parents had consistently told her, "Julia, you have a gift. A gift for learning that God has bestowed upon you. Now, you have an obligation to use that gift to help others." Julia always took her gift very seriously, but she couldn't help but feel a twinge of guilt for the blessings of intelligence she had received while her beloved brother Mikey struggled so mightily. Consequently, when Julia's PhD program began, she knew that she would use her studies to help those who had difficulty learning. After soliciting her mentor, Dr. Lawrence, for advice, the choice began to crystallize right in front of her.

"Julia," Dr. Lawrence began, "you have shown such promise in your career to date. And if I'm hearing you correctly, the decision seems like an obvious one. Let me recap... You're interested in psychiatry to help individuals emotionally as well as physically. You're interested in learning. And finally, you'd like to help those that have difficulty with the acquisition of knowledge. Is this correct?"

"Yes," Julia responded. "You have summed up my sentiments perfectly."

Dr. Lawrence raised his brow and his eyes lit up. "Well young lady, I have two words for you... School Psychology! It is a noble profession, one in which the Psychologist or the Psychiatrist uses his, or in this case her, abilities to help the student succeed in school. Whether that be emotionally or academically, the student is the Psychiatrist's number one priority."

"That sounds fascinating!" Julia beamed.

"And furthermore," Dr. Lawrence continued, "the area of learning disabilities is an exciting arena with a real chance to make a difference for those students who are having unexplained difficulties leaning."

"It sounds perfect," a young, idealistic Julia shot back. "Where do I sign up?" That conversation was nearly twenty years ago, but Julia still credits it as being the pivotal moment of her professional career. And now, getting ready for her abnormal psychiatry lecture at Yale, she was looking forward toward the future. But in reality Dr. Julia Pearlman only ever looked forward. She never looked back.

CHAPTER 5

William Victory was having what appeared to be a carbon copy conversation with his guidance counselor, Mrs. Cone. Sandy Cone was an experienced guidance counselor with over twenty-five years of high school experience under her belt. Although she had seen countless unmotivated students come through her office somehow William was slightly different, yet she couldn't quite put her finger on why. Sure he was bright, but she had seen other intelligent unmotivated students. No, somehow William was special. But things were getting desperate, and Mrs. Cone had had enough.

"William," she stammered, "we just don't know what we're going to do with you anymore. I've told you a thousand times, you need to get your act together! And now your D's are turning into F's. At this rate I'm afraid you're not going to graduate with your classmates. Well… what do you have to say for yourself, young man?" William sat motionless on the metal chair in Mrs. Cone's cramped office, not saying a word.

"Well?" Mrs. Cone asked again, obviously frustrated. "Do you have any answers for me? Because frankly I'm tired of asking the same questions." Another few seconds ticked away quietly until William finally cleared his throat.

"I think I do have an answer for you, Mrs. Cone." Another moment of silence passed.

"Please William, enlighten me," Mrs. Cone answered somewhat sarcastically.

And then William dropped his bombshell. "I've decided to drop out of school."

It took a lot to shock Sandy Cone, but this was one of those times. She didn't see this one coming. She just sat there in shocked speechlessness for a few seconds before finally composing herself. "William, you can't be serious. You're so close to graduating. I know I've been hard on you but don't you think you can stick it out for just one more year until you graduate?"

"What would be the point?" a defeated looking William quietly replied.

"For one thing, you'd have a high school diploma. All of those 'cruel world' speeches I gave you weren't for nothing. It's the truth, and without a diploma in your hand the odds of success shoot right down the drain. Just tell me why, William. Throughout all of our meetings you've never opened up to me. I know things are tough at home. Is that it? Does it have something to do with your home life? Please William, I really want to help. Please, please, please, all I'm asking is that you just tell me why." William just sat there with his head in his hands. After what seemed like an eternity he finally looked up to see a very concerned Mrs. Cone. But when Mrs. Cone returned his stare she was shocked to see a tear running down this troubled student's face. Another moment of excruciating silence.

"Please William, confide in me. I'm here for you." William's mind was racing, but he had a feeling that if he didn't take this chance now he might regret it for the rest of his life. He mustered up his strength and decided to lay it all on the line. *What the hell,* he thought, *I'll probably never see her again anyway.*

"You know all of those times you told me that I'm smart and I just need to try harder?"

"Yes," she answered.

"Well, I'm not. Actually, I'm stupid!" he said almost angrily. "All of these years when everybody thought I was just goofing around I've actually been working my ass off, and I got D's anyway. I've had it, Mrs. Cone. I'll always be stupid, with or without a piece of paper telling me I've graduated. So I figure, screw it! Why waste any more of my time? I mean, I'll never amount to anything anyhow." For years William had been thinking these thoughts, and it felt like a weight was being lifted off his shoulders. Finally... the truth. For a fleeting moment he actually felt relieved.

"William, I had no idea," Sandy said, now fighting her own tears. "You've actually been working... working hard..." her voice trailed off.

"Yeah, and that's how I know everyone's been wrong about me. You see Mrs. Cone, I'm not smart like everyone says. I'm an idiot!"

Sandy Cone knew that if she was going to save this student she had better do some fast talking, and her years of experience took over. "Listen William, and listen carefully. For years we all thought you simply weren't trying, but now that I know the truth I can go to the S.A.T. That stands for the 'Student Assistance Team.' It's a team of teachers, regular and special education as well as administrators, who work on modifications and accommodations for students who are motivated but simply are not cutting it in school. William, there are many reasons why students don't succeed besides a lack of intelligence, and I can tell you with the utmost confidence that you are not stupid. Just give me one more month, and if the school can't come up with a suitable plan then I'll walk you out the front door myself." William looked doubtful, and Sandy sensed it. "Just one month, that's all I'm asking for."

"OK, one month. But I'm telling you it won't do any good. I appreciate what you're trying to do for me Mrs. Cone, I really do, but believe me when I tell you that I'm a lost cause. You can go to all the Student Assistance Team meetings in the state but when it comes down to it I'm just a big fat dummy!"

CHAPTER 6

Julia was sitting in an oversized black leather chair as her patient lamented on his current sad state of affairs while lying on the matching sofa.

"I don't know what it is, Dr. Pearlman. I think I just have an overactive libido or something. I see these beautiful women and I just have to have them." As a small smirk arose on the lips of this small, disdainful man of Mediterranean descent, Julia reminded herself to keep her clinical judgment.

"Have you thought about sharing this information with your new bride, Mr. Vito?"

"You know I can't do that, Doctor. She'd leave me faster than a New York minute. And as they say, what she don't know won't hurt me." As Anthony Vito let out a small chuckle Julia fought herself from rolling her eyes. Julia's mind began to drift as she thought to herself, *Why did I have to waste my time with such infantile behavior when there are people out there in serious need of psychological services?* She contemplated the answer. If she wanted to make a difference through her research and her teaching position, not to mention taking care of her brother, she would have to make some compromises. In this case that meant charging this swine $200 per hour in order to subsidize her other low paying, more altruistic endeavors.

"Well Mr. Vito, we've been working together for several months now and it seems to me that we've been going in circles."

"What do ya mean, Doc? I feel like I'm making real progress here. Just last week I decided not to sleep with Roxanne anymore. Plus, she ain't that hot anyway." This insensitive statement was once again followed by an infantile laugh.

"But Mr. Vito," an exasperated Julia answered, "you're still having affairs with three other women."

"Yeah, that's true and all, but Doc, these girls are real lookers I tell ya. What do you think my problem is, Dr. Pearlman? Am I just that irresistible?" Another chuckle.

"Well, clinically I must determine that you fall under the category of a sex addict. But the good news is that there's hope. With some hard work, real commitment and a willingness to change, many sex addicts go on to live happy, monogamous lives."

"That all sounds great Doc, except for the hard work, commitment and willingness to change part." With this last caveat Anthony Vito almost fell off the sofa laughing.

At this a defeated Dr. Pearlman looked at her clock on the wall and thankfully stated, "Our time is up for today, Mr. Vito. I'll walk you out."

Julia and Anthony began to walk toward the door of her office, which led into the main portion of her house. Yet as they entered the living room Julia and Mr. Vito were in for a shock - a shock Julia had encountered before. Mikey greeted the two of them with a sing song rendition of "Sex Addict, Sex Addict, Sex Addict" as he pointed at a humiliated, red faced Anthony Vito.

"Mikey, that's enough!" Julia shouted. "I'm so sorry, Mr. Vito. I've talked to my brother about listening at the door while I'm in a session in the past. I'm terribly sorry," Julia apologized.

"You mean this retard has done this before?" a now angry Anthony shouted.

"Mr. Vito, I know you're upset, and understandably so, but please refrain from using that type of language. It's very insulting."

"Well, he started it!" Anthony sputtered. "And I'll tell ya something else, this is the last time you'll see me again! How does that make your wallet feel?"

"Well Mr. Vito, I'm sorry you feel this way, but under the circumstances I think it's best that you leave."

"I knew this head shrinking crap was for the birds. See ya, and I wouldn't want to be ya!" And with that a very disgruntled patient slammed the door and stormed out.

CHAPTER 7

Sandy Cone had been to literally thousands of Student Assistance Team meetings over her twenty-five years as a guidance counselor, but as she entered the assistant principal's office on this crisp fall afternoon she felt a nervous determination envelope her. The S.A.T. was made up of two special education teachers, two regular education teachers, one guidance counselor (Mrs. Cone), and headed by the assistant principle, Mr. Falk. The purpose of the S.A.T. was to identify students who may be struggling in the school setting, whether that be academically, socially or emotionally, and to attempt to aid the student in their area of need. The normal protocol was to first try regular education interventions. If these efforts proved unsuccessful the special education department would then make a determination as to whether or not the student in question was eligible for special education services. This was normally done through a battery of tests.

Benjamin Falk was a no-nonsense administrator that didn't like to waste time. Yet despite his at times abrupt demeanor, he had the respect of the faculty for the sole reason that he simply cared about the students. When Ben Falk made a decision you could bet that it was with the student's best interest at heart. As the teachers milled into the cramped office and made small talk, Mr. Falk, always aware of the adage 'too much to do, too little time,' brought the meeting succinctly to order.

"Good afternoon people. I know it's Friday afternoon and our thoughts are probably on our weekend plans, but as you know time is short, so let's please get started." As papers around the table began to shuffle, Mr. Falk's secretary, Mrs. Scherzo, began to read the minutes. As is normal protocol, the committee members first reviewed the current S.A.T. cases that were deemed to be in dire need. After several minutes of discussion they moved on to the students who were currently being serviced and seemed to be making progress. Again, several minutes of discussion ensued as Mrs. Cone impatiently tapped her pencil. As the meeting progressed Sandy Cone showed all the signs of being a caged lion by shifting uncomfortably in her chair and sighing loudly, to the consternation of some of her colleagues. Finally, with several minutes left in the period, Mr. Falk made the announcement. "Does anyone have any new students they would like to recommend to the S.A.T.?"

At this Sandy stood up so abruptly that she actually knocked the chair over behind her. "Sandy, is everything OK?" the teacher next to her asked worriedly.

"I'm sorry," Sandy gushed. "It's just that I'm very worried about one of my students."

"That's OK," Mr. Falk answered. "Just take a second to catch your breath, then tell us what's got you so fired up."

Sandy inhaled deeply through her nose, then she began. "I'm

sure many of you know William Victory." Several heads nodded. "Well, he's considering dropping out of school, and it's got me very upset. For three years I've been dogging him to get his act together and to start applying himself. It's obvious to me that he's a bright kid but he's been getting D's all through high school, until recently where he's been receiving F's."

"I have him in class," his biology teacher interjected. "He never hands in his homework and is almost always unprepared for quizzes and tests."

"Well, would you believe that until recently he's been spending hours a night studying in vain and simply can't understand the material? The reason he doesn't hand in his homework is because he simply can't complete it. And the reason he is doing so poorly on his tests isn't due to a lack of effort but simply due to the fact that he just doesn't get it, no matter how hard he bangs his head against the wall."

"Are you sure, Sandy?" one of the special education teachers asked her. "I mean, I don't have to tell you how many times I've heard 'I'm trying my best' even though it's obvious the student hasn't picked up a book in months."

"Believe me," Sandy shot back, "it's the first thing that ran through my mind. But I know William pretty well, and he's not one to lie. And if you had seen him in my office you'd know he was telling the truth. It's just got me so upset. I've been riding him for years, and he's been trying the whole time," Sandy chided herself.

At this point Mr. Falk jumped in. "So we have a student who is apparently bright and motivated, until late anyway, who hasn't been cutting it. Normally we would try some modifications to his program, but he is a senior…"

"And he's ready to drop out of school any minute," Sandy interjected.

"So what do you recommend we do, Sandy? You know this student better than any of us."

"I think we have to go to testing immediately. There's simply no time for modifying his program. By the time we find a change in his routine that may work he'll be out of here. I think we need to get to the heart of the problem immediately. And with all due respect to the staff here at JFK, I think we need some outside help - an expert that can cut through all of the red tape and get right to the heart of the matter. If William is to be saved we need to do something immediately!"

"Sandy, I think I know where you're heading. You know we only have her one day every two weeks, and she's already tapped out," Mr. Falk explained.

"I know," Sandy responded. "But I think this is one of those special situations in which drastic measures are justified. If this student is to be saved it will take swift action and an expert diagnostician - it will take Dr. Pearlman!"

CHAPTER 8

Early Monday morning Julia was in her lab at Yale with her favorite furry friend Sigmund, named for Julia's favorite psychological figure, Sigmund Freud. Siggy, as Julia called him, was a white hamster who initially had no difficulty learning. In fact, this hamster had originally been at the top of his class, performing better than ninety-five percent of his cohort. But, after a series of electroconvulsive shocks to Sigmund's frontal cortex (utilized to induce a simulated learning disability), it now took him nearly fifty percent longer than the typical hamster to maneuver his way through the maze used to decipher cognitive efficiency. However, thanks to several intelligence-enhancing drugs surging through his cortex, Sigmund was now maneuvering his way through the maze as well as or better than twenty-two percent of the other hamsters in her study. While there was some improvement, it wasn't nearly what Julia had hoped for.

After years of research Julia felt that there must be a link between neurotransmitters (the chemicals in the brain that carry electrical impulses from one neuron to the next) and intellectual ability. But finding just the right amount of each neurotransmitting agent to optimize one's cognitive functioning was proving to be a most formidable task, to say the least. *Maybe if I just increase the amount of neuroepinephrine, or decrease the amount serotonin, that would be the answer*, she surmised. Julia had played the game of 'what if' for so long that she worried she may never find the answer.

Julia was lost in thought when the ringing telephone brought her back to reality. "Hello, this is Julia," she answered.

"Hi Julia, it's Ben Falk from JFK. I'm sorry to bother you at work."

"It's no bother Ben, what can I do for you?"

"Well Julia, first of all I just want to express again how much all of us at JFK appreciate your help. For you to volunteer your time and expertise to an under-funded school system such as ours in truly invaluable."

"I appreciate you saying that Ben but we've had this conversation before, and as you know I love working with the kids and I'm happy to do it. Plus, it seems like every time I'm there I learn something new, so it's really my pleasure. So, what can I do for you?"

"Well, I know how busy your schedule is, but we have an interesting case that needs immediate attention."

"I'm listening…"

"A senior by the name of William Victory is contemplating dropping out of school. He's a seemingly bright boy but is barely scraping by despite considerable effort. The school has decided to bypass the usual in-school modifications and go right to testing."

"Why is that?" Julia inquired.

"We feel that if we wait with this student he'll drop out and there will be no saving him. Even though we obviously don't want to see any of our students fail, this boy seems to be unusually special."

"How so?" Julia asked as she leaned forward in her seat.

"Not only does he appear to be bright, but he's a very likable kid with a terrible home life. If he drops out there's really no future for him," Ben surmised.

Julia couldn't help but feel for William, even though she had never met him. She had always felt that she was so fortunate to come from such a loving family. She knew deep down that without all of the support she had received she wouldn't be half the person she was today, not to mention that her brother Mikey would probably be in an institution if not for the around-the-clock support he received. Julia just couldn't stand to see wasted potential.

"What can I do to help?" Julia asked sincerely.

"If you could find the time to do some testing with William and try to get to the bottom of why he is having so much academic difficulty it would be greatly appreciated. And Julia, time is of the essence."

"I'll see him before the week is over."

CHAPTER 9

Two days after her conversation with Ben Falk, Julia was in his office. "Hi Ben. How are we today?" Julia said with a wry smile.

"I'm doing much better now that you're here. I take it you've come to spend some time with our friend?"

"Just find me a quiet cubby hole to work in and William and I will take it from there."

"I'll have my secretary call him down to the office."

About three minutes later William made his way into the assistant principal's office where Ben and Julia stood to meet him. "Hi William," Mr. Falk began. "This is the woman Mrs. Cone was telling you about."

"Hello, William. I'm Dr. Pearlman."

"Uh, hi," William said, keeping he gaze glued to the floor. Julia, sensing William's apprehension, decided to try and break the ice.

"William, I was hoping we could do some work together and

try to figure out just exactly why you're having such a tough time in school. And William, I've got some good news - I don't bite." At this attempt at levity William finally looked up to see Dr. Pearlman wearing a genuine smile and found that he couldn't suppress an almost imperceptible smile of his own.

With the tension easing Ben Falk jumped in. "Well, if you two are ready to get started, I've managed to secure a small room across from the guidance office."

"What do you say, William?" Julia asked with another smile. "I'm ready if you are."

"I guess I'm all set," William said, and with that they were off.

Several minutes later Julia was sitting across from William in what felt like a closet to Julia. "When Mr. Falk said we were going to a small room I guess he wasn't kidding," Julia said with an amused tone.

"I guess there ain't much space at this school," William said.

"Well we'll just make the best of it," Julia said with an attitude that William couldn't help but find a little contagious. "Before we begin, I just want you to know that I'm confident we're going to get to the bottom of your difficulties. All you have to do is give it your best effort. So what do you say? Can we give it a shot?"

"I'll do my best Dr. Pearlman, but…" William's voice trailed off.

"What is it, William?" Silence filled the room. "There are two things you should know," Julia began. "First, everything we do together is confidential unless you give me permission to share it with others. And second, if we're to make any real progress you need to know that you can say anything to me and I promise I won't be judgmental. So please, what is it you want to say?"

William looked at Julia's caring face and somehow just sensed that he could trust her. "Dr. Pearlman, I appreciate everything you're trying to do for me, but I'm telling you right up front that it's a waste of time."

"Why's that?" Julia asked.

"Cause I'm just a dummy, and no test is gonna make me smart."

"Well do me a favor, William - just do your best for the next couple of hours, and I promise you I'll be honest with the results. If the test says that you just don't have the smarts for high school, I promise I'll tell it like it is. All you have to do is give me a couple of hours of your best effort. Do we have a deal?"

"I've got nothing better to do," William said with a defeated tone. And with that Julia pulled out the testing materials and began what would be an astonishing few hours.

CHAPTER 10

The first subtest of the cognitive protocol evaluated visual-spatial skills. Julia pulled several blocks out of her bag, along with her stopwatch. She showed William a picture of a three dimensional block design and asked William to recreate it as fast as he could. Generally all of the intellectual subtests started off with the easy items first and became progressively more difficult. Consequently, when William cruised through the first couple of block patterns Julia was not surprised. However, as the testing continued to become more difficult Julia had to fight to control her astonishment. The testing protocol was very explicit - the tester was not permitted to let the subject know how he or she was doing under any circumstances until the testing was completely finished. But when William finished every block pattern correctly and in a very efficient manner, Julia's face began to contort uncontrollably. William, noticing Julia's exasperation, couldn't help but feel disappointed.

"I'm doin' that bad, huh?" William asked.

"What do you mean?" Julia asked.

"I can tell by the expression on your face. I can see you trying not to show it, but it's obvious I'm doin' bad."

"William, I'm sorry if I'm giving you that impression, but remember what I told you before we started? Just do your best for a couple of hours and I promise that I'll tell it like it is. Deal?"

"I guess," a discouraged William consented.

As the testing progressed William continued to amaze Julia. His receptive and expressive verbal skills were phenomenal, his perceptual visual skills were off the chart, and his short term auditory memory and abstract reasoning were the best Julia had ever seen. As the testing ended William seemed oblivious to the fact that he had just aced the assessment.

"William, how do you think you did?" Julia asked, trying to contain her enthusiasm.

"Probably pretty bad. I mean, even I could tell that this is some sort of brain ability test, right?"

"Yes, William. You just took a test of intellectual ability, otherwise known as an IQ test."

"I betcha it will show you that I'm an idiot," William said as he stood up.

"Well William, we should know soon enough. I'm going to go back to my office and score your results, and I should have an IQ score for you within the next couple of weeks."

"I can't wait," William said sarcastically.

"I don't want to get your hopes up William, but I've given this test countless times and I can't remember anyone doing as well as you."

William gave her a look of disbelief. "Just wait 'til you score it, Dr. Pearlman. I bet you I'm not as smart as you're guessing."

"We'll see," Julia said. And with that William walked out of the room and back to another frustrating day of school.

CHAPTER II

Julia broke several traffic laws getting back to her office. She threw her purse on her desk and rushed to turn her computer on. "Come on, come on," she muttered impatiently as her computer slowly booted up. Julia raced through the protocol as she entered William's answers into the computer. She was so excited that she actually began to glisten with sweat. As Julia submitted the last of William's answers the computer prompted her to 'Please press enter to obtain the results.' Julia pressed enter and held her breath. 'Please wait approximately ten seconds while the computer compiles the results.' Julia felt her heart flutter. Although she had performed countless intellectual assessments, this one was different. She knew that William had done well, but how well?

The computer started with a standard statement: 'The average Intellectual Quotient is 100. Please scroll down to see the subject's results.' Julia gasped as she quickly moved the cursor down.
"Oh my God!" she said aloud. She rubbed her eyes and looked again. '**142**.' "He's a bonafide genius!" Julia nearly screamed.

CHAPTER 12

The next morning William was once again called down to Mr. Falk's office, and once again he saw Julia waiting with him. Yet this time William sensed something was amiss. As he studied the two faces in the office William couldn't help but feel that Ben and Julia were laughing at him. They each had a seemingly silly smile on their face, and they were looking right at him. *Could I be so stupid that they're actually laughing at me?* a paranoid William thought.

"Hello William," Mr. Falk began. "How are you feeling today?" he said with a big toothy grin.

"I'm not sure... OK I guess."

"Well I'm sure you're surprised to see Dr. Pearlman again so soon, but she has some news she couldn't wait to share with you. So without further ado, Dr. Pearlman, you have the floor."

"Well William, I came back to see you today because I couldn't wait to share the results of your testing. Although we use the results of this assessment for several purposes, such as defining your strengths and weaknesses, it is first and foremost an intelligence test." As William listened intently to Dr. Pearlman he couldn't help but sense the worst. Julia was too excited to notice, so she continued. "An average IQ score is 100, and your score is..." She stood up for effect. "Tadaa, 142!"

"What'd you say?" a startled William asked.

"That's right William, 142. You scored off the charts! In reality it's the highest score I've ever seen. You're an outright genius!"

"There's gotta be a mistake, Dr. Pearlman. I mean, if I'm so smart how come I'm failing?" William said with a look of disbelief. "Mr. Falk, tell her how bad I do at school."

"I assure you there is no mistake," Julia continued. "The score is accurate. The reason you're having such difficulty is due to a learning disability."

"A what?" William asked.

"You have what's called a learning disability. Let me explain," Julia said as she sat back down. "A typical student, with effort and afforded the chance, will work up to their ability level. However, certain people's brains are simply wired differently from the average population. They are no better or worse, simply different. Consequently, the standard style of teaching given to the general population is usually inadequate to fill the needs of a learning disabled, or L.D. student. Therefore, a person with a learning disability will need to learn certain compensatory methods in order to tap into their true potential. You see William, you have great cognitive abilities, you just have to learn to utilize them."

"And how do I do that?" William asked.

"That's a good question. Maybe you would like to answer that, Mr. Falk."

"I'd be happy to. You see William, we have specially trained teachers called special education teachers that are specifically prepared to help students that are similar to you. At this point the testing that you and Dr. Pearlman went through has qualified you as a special education student and you are now eligible to receive these services."

At this William jumped out of his seat. "What are you guys trying to pull here?" William stated, his voice getting louder. "First you tell me I'm some kind of an Einstein and then you put me in the retard class." Julia cringed when she heard William refer to special education as a 'retard class' and quickly cut him off to rebut his point.

"William, let me make one thing perfectly clear. Special education is not only for retards, as you put it. Students are enrolled in special education services for a variety of reasons. In fact, many learning disabled students have above average IQ's. So please, get it out of your head that you're stupid because it's simply not true. I want you to listen to me very carefully, and try to let this sink in. You're smart, William. You're very, very smart."

CHAPTER 13

As always, William waited for his girlfriend Maria by the exit door at the end of the school day. Maria was not considered by most to be a classic beauty - she was short with dark curly hair and glasses. Yet her petite stature and shy personality made her endearing to all who knew her, and most importantly, William and Maria loved each other. Although Maria wasn't particularly bright, William begrudgingly admitted to himself that this was one of his favorite characteristics of his beloved. Around Maria, William never felt stupid, never felt inadequate. As William recounted the details of his meeting earlier in the day Maria could hardly believe it.

"You're really a genius, Will? I mean I guess I always knew you weren't stupid, but really… a genius?"

"I know, it's hard to believe. Jesus, I still don't really believe it myself, but that's what these people are telling me." William and Maria continued to walk down the street of broken-down apartment buildings until they finally came to William's place of residence. "Can you come up for a while?" William asked.

"Who am I to turn down a genius?" Maria said with a cute little laugh. As the two lovebirds made their way into the apartment they walked in on an all-too-common scene. There on the torn sofa lay William's mother, beer cans strewn about, passed out drunk. William looked to Maria, who tried not to look uncomfortable but clearly was.

"I guess I should take her to the bedroom," William said. As he lifted his mother up like an infant she began to wake up.

"Who's that?" she slurred.

"It's me, mom. William."

"What the hell do you think you're doin'?"

"I'm just taking you to bed to sleep it off."

"What the hell do you mean 'sleep it off,' you condescending SOB. I'm fine, damn it! Now put me down!" William slowly lowered his mother to the floor and she stumbled back to the sofa. "What the hell are you doing here, anyway?" she slobbered.

"School's over, ma. It's three o'clock in the afternoon. Why aren't you at work?"

"Because my boss is an asshole! He caught me having a little drinky-drink on the job and that uptight loser fired me. So I say the hell with him!"

"But what are we going to do for money, mom?"

"I'll get another job. I mean, hell, I always do. But I don't want to talk about that moronic job anymore. It was beneath me anyway. What happened at school today?" Mary Victory asked, her eyes half shut.

"Nothin' really."

"What do you mean nothing!" an excited Maria exclaimed. "Will got some very exciting news today, Mrs. Victory." As

William shot Maria a 'be quiet' look Mary's ears perked up.

"Well William, what's so exciting?" William remained silent for several seconds, so Mary persisted. "Come on Willy, tell me. How come you never share anything with your mama?" she slurred.

"Well ma," an apprehensive William began, "this doctor lady did some testing on me, and they tell me I'm smart."

"What's that?" a half comatose Mary asked.

"The doctor gave me an IQ test and they told me I'm a genius."

At this news Mary couldn't control herself and began laughing uncontrollably. "You, a genius?! Is this the same kid who comes home with all D's? And monkey's are gonna fly out of my ass," Mary spewed with a combination of spit and laughter. And with that Mary fell off the sofa and onto the floor, passing out once again.

CHAPTER 14

Over the next several months William gave his best effort in school. Now enrolled in special education classes, William was cautiously optimistic that things would be better. Yet despite extraordinary efforts on the part of William's new teachers, the results were unfortunately the same. No matter what techniques the teachers used and no matter how hard William tried he just couldn't seem to overcome his learning difficulties. Now, with less than one semester left in his senior year, William found himself once again in the office of Sandy Cone.

"I just can't do it Mrs. Cone," a disheartened William explained. "These new special classes just don't help."

"But William, it's only been a couple of months," Sandy argued. "Don't you think you could stick it out until the end of the year?"

"I really don't. I'm just sick of sitting in these classes and feeling like an idiot. I just ain't gettin' it!"

"But William, what are you going to do without a high school diploma? How are you going to get a job?"

"I don't know, but to tell you the truth I really don't care. With or without a stupid piece of paper telling me I graduated I'll always be stupid."

"That's simply not true, William. You know what Dr. Pearlman said." At this statement the normally subdued William became visibly angry.

"You know what Mrs. Cone, I'm sick and tired of people telling me I'm smart, cause I'm not! I appreciate what everyone is trying to do for me but you're all wastin' your time. You're wastin' your time and I'm wastin' mine. That's it..." William announced more than said. "I've had enough. I'm sorry Mrs. Cone, I really am, but I quit. Just tell me where to sign and I'm out of here." At that a defeated Sandy Cone knew the battle was over. She reached into her dreaded bottom drawer to get the appropriate paperwork.

CHAPTER 15

As William made his way out of the building for the final time, a frantic Sandy Cone rushed by Mr. Falk's secretary and barged into his office. A surprised Ben was in the middle of a meeting with another teacher, but Sandy would not be deterred. "I'm sorry Ben, but this can't wait."

"I'm afraid we'll have to reschedule this conference, Mrs. Montgomery," Ben said, half annoyed and half concerned. "What is it, Sandy? Where's the fire?"

"William Victory just dropped out of school!" an exasperated Sandy explained. "I tried to talk him into sticking it out until the end of the year but he wouldn't be deterred."

Ben Falk put his hand to his forehead. "Damn it," he nearly whispered. "Are you sure there's no way to convince him to finish out the school year?"

"I don't think so," Sandy stated as she plopped down onto a chair. "I'm just so upset, Ben. This boy is special, and now he's really got a bleak future in front of him. Isn't there anything we can do?"

"We'll I've got one idea," Ben said. "It's kind of a long shot, but it's worth a try."

CHAPTER 16

Julia had just come home from a long day of teaching at Yale. After two cognitive psychology lectures and supervising an abnormal psychology lab, not to mention her own research and office hours, Julia was exhausted. She came home to find Mikey watching cartoons on the sofa. "Hey there Mikey," Julia said, trying to muster up some energy. "How was your day at the grocery store?"

Mikey had been working at the local grocerette for about a decade as a bagger and generally enjoyed doing the work. Apparently he was too engrossed in his cartoon to even notice Julia and remained silent. "Earth to Mikey, come in Mikey," Julia teased.

"Oh hi Julie," Mikey finally responded, barely turning his head from the television. "I'm hungry." Julia looked at her watch and couldn't believe it was almost eight o'clock. Where had the day gone?

"I'm sorry, Mikey. I didn't realize how late it had gotten. What would you like for dinner?"

"Peanut butter and jelly... Peanut butter and jelly," Mikey sang. Julia, who was an excellent cook, normally insisted on a more substantial meal, but tonight she simply didn't have the energy to argue.

"OK Mikey, let me just check the messages and I'll whip it up in a jiffy."

Julia was delighted to see that she only had one message on the machine. Unfortunately, the message was slightly disconcerting.

"Hi Julia, it's Ben Falk from JFK. I'm sorry to bother you at home, but I called your office at Yale and they told me you were in a lecture, and I really needed to contact you today. Can you give me a call back as soon as you get this? Feel free to call me at home tonight - you can call as late as you want. The number is 555-6657. Thanks Julia... Bye."

Julia sensed that it must be bad news if Ben wanted her to call him at home. She quickly made Mikey his sandwich, poured him a glass of milk, then went to her office to call Ben. After two rings he picked up the phone. "Hi Ben, it's Julia. I hope I'm not calling too late."

"It's not too late at all. I was hoping you'd have a chance to call me back tonight."

"What can I help you with?"

"Unfortunately I have some bad news. William Victory just dropped out of school, and it's got us all pretty upset."

"What? Did he say why?" Julia inquired.

"Actually he did. Despite all of the efforts from the special education department he's just not able to learn. He feels inadequate, and consequently isn't even willing to stick it out for one more semester to obtain his high school diploma."

"That's terrible," Julia said, shaking her head. "What a waste."

"Furthermore, he's got no support at home and now nobody he can rely on besides his girlfriend, Maria. And between you and me Julia, even though Maria is a sweet girl I don't think she's capable of giving him the support that he needs."

"And that's where I come in," Julia said, smiling.

"Well, we here at JFK were hoping so. You've been known to pick up a pro-bono case from time to time, and I know it's asking a lot, but…"

Julia cut him off. "I'd be happy to Ben. I know I only met him a couple of times, but to be honest he really had an impact on me, and not just because of his genius IQ. There's just something… special about him."

"I'm so glad you see it too," Ben chimed in. "He's a very likable kid, but without some professional guidance I don't see him making it."

"Do you think he'd be willing to come for counseling?" Julia asked.

"Well now that I know you're willing to see him at least I can call him at home and ask him to go. I'll give him a call first thing tomorrow and let you know as soon as I hear something. And Julia?" Ben said, gushing. "I don't know what we'd do without you… Thank you."

"It's truly my pleasure, Ben."

CHAPTER 17

It took about twenty minutes of cajoling, but due to the fact that William sincerely respected Mr. Falk (and the fact that William could tell he was not going to take no for an answer), William finally acquiesced and agreed to meet with Julia. After a couple of calls back and forth Ben finally mediated a meeting for Julia and William on Saturday morning. The doorbell rang promptly at eight o'clock that morning. Julia was happy to see that William was able to make it on time at such an early hour on the weekend. In reality Julia had needed to schedule William so early due to her packed schedule, but she always liked to see her unmotivated clients at unseemly hours for their first visit. Julia surmised that if they were willing to make an effort to be on time for an inconvenient appointment, then there was hope that they'd be willing to try during therapy.

William showed up in jeans, a sweatshirt and a baseball cap that looked like it had been through the ringer. "Hello William,"

Julia chirped. "I'm so happy that you were willing to meet with me."

"To be honest I don't think it'll do any good, but Mr. Falk asked me to give it a try."

"I appreciate your honesty, William. My office is through the house, this way." As Julia led William through the foyer and then the living room she stopped to introduce him to Mikey, who was once again on the sofa watching cartoons.

"Mikey, can you take your eyes off of the television for just a second? I want you to meet someone."

Mikey turned around to look at the two of them. "Mikey, this is my friend William. Can you say hi?"

"Hi William. My name's Mikey," he said with a contagious grin. Surprisingly Julia noticed William visibly perk up, and she stood there slightly shocked as he began a dialogue with her brother.

"Hi there Mikey, what'er you watchin'?"

"The Flintstones," Mikey said.

William took a look at the television. "I've seen this one. It's one of my favorites."

"Me too," Mikey said excitedly.

"Who's your favorite character?" William asked, as if he really wanted to know the answer.

"I like Barney," Mikey chuckled. "He's so funny."

"I like him too. Maybe we can watch it together sometime," William said sincerely.

"That'd be great!" Mikey said, his grin now turning into a full-fledged smile. Julia couldn't believe how such a reserved William had opened up with her brother, and she was truly moved.

"OK you two. I hate to break this up, but William and I need to talk for a little while. If there's time at the end maybe you two can watch together for a few minutes, OK?"

"Can you William, can you?" Mikey begged.

"You can count on it," William said, giving Mikey a wink.

As William and Julia sat down to begin, Julia looked at William with genuine respect. "William, I want to thank you for being so kind to my brother. You'd be amazed but a lot of people get very uncomfortable around him, and you were just so at ease."

"He seems like a great guy," William stated, very matter-of-fact.

"He really is, but if you're too busy to watch cartoons with him believe me I'll understand."

"I've got nothing else to do. I'm a high school dropout, remember?" William stated self-loathingly.

"Well maybe that's a good place for us to get started." Julia leaned forward in her chair and addressed William, who was now seated uncomfortably on the couch. "There are two things that I want you to know. First of all, like I told you the first time we met, everything we talk about together in strictly confidential. And secondly, I'm here to do my best to help you. So please feel free to tell me whatever comes to your mind, and know that I'm not here to judge but to help." William looked Julia right in the eyes and nodded his understanding. "Now William, I normally like to begin by getting to know my clients, so can you tell me a little bit about yourself?"

"There ain't much to tell, really. I'm basically just a loser."

"Why do you say that William? From what everyone at JFK told me you're a very likable young man."

"Well for one thing I've got like no friends... besides my girlfriend, that is. I live with my ma who's worse off than me, and worst of all I'm stupid. And please Dr. Pearlman, please don't tell me how smart that test says I am because it just ain't true." The fifty minute session followed suit with Julia asking questions and William putting himself down. Julia couldn't help but see great promise in William but knew that without a strong support system he would never even come close to reaching his potential.

As time expired for the day Julia found herself liking William more and more and truly wanted to help him. "William, that's all the time we have for today, but if it's alright with you I'd like to spend some more time with you and see if we can get you back on track."

William surprised himself by answering, "That would be OK I guess." For when the truth was told, William not only liked Julia but knew that she was the only chance he had. As Julia led William out of the office William shocked Julia once again by asking, "Do you mind if I hang out with Mikey for a while?"

"I'd really appreciate that, William."

William spent the next hour sitting with Mikey, talking to him and truly listening to him before he finally got up quietly and walked out the door, back to his miserable existence.

CHAPTER 18

Julia and William continued to meet every Saturday for the next several months. Although some progress was being made, it was slow and painstaking. Julia was beginning to come to the realization that William's severe learning disability would forever plague him, for despite all of his issues his lack of intellectual confidence was at the root of his problems. Although Julia had great respect for special education and had seen firsthand the marvels that it could work, she was convinced that for severe cases such as William they needed a greater intervention. The wiring in those unlucky few was so convoluted that the brain chemistry had to be altered. Of this she was certain. Consequently, with William as her newfound inspiration, she threw herself back into her research and was spending more time than ever at her lab.

"I'm sorry to do this to you again, Siggy," Julia said, once again injecting her prize hamster with 10cc's of her most recent mixture of a neurotransmiting agent. Although Sigmund continued to make cerebral progress Julia just knew in her heart of hearts that with the right formula a large breakthrough could be made that would translate into humans. Julia drummed her fingers absentmindedly on the large metal lab table and surmised her current position for the countless time. *What haven't I thought of? What other possibilities are out there? For William and the multitude of others suffering, I've just got to make a breakthrough... I've just got to.*

CHAPTER 19

As William and Julia sat in her office on a beautiful spring day the mood in the room was anything but cheery. "My Ma wants me out of the house," William said, shrugging his shoulders. "I don't know what I'm gonna do now."

"Are you making enough money to get your own place?"

"No, and to make things worse I just lost my job... again," William said, an embarrassed look painted across his face.

"I'm sorry, William. What happened this time?" Julia asked, although she full well knew the answer.

"Same thing as always. My boss said he just can't count on me to get things done. And to tell ya the truth, I don't blame him. I can't do nothing right. And the weird part is the harder I try the worse I screw it up," a dejected William explained. This was the third job William had lost in the last two months.

"Have you applied for unemployment?"

"Yeah. It's getting easier each time. I'm becoming an expert."

This attempt at levity broke the tension and both William and Julia let out a small chuckle, if just for a moment. "There has to be a job even an idiot like me can do. Do you have any ideas Dr. Pearlman?" Julia leaned back in her chair and breathed deeply. She had contemplated this moment for some time but had reservations due to the complexities of the doctor-patient relationship. After thinking for a moment, Julia decided to just go for it.

"I can ask over at Yale if there's anything if you'd like, but I don't want to make any promises."

"That'd be great. I'd appreciate it," William said, perking up a little. "In the meantime Maria and I have been talkin', and we've decided to shack up together."

"That's a big step, William. Are you sure you're both ready for such a big commitment?" Julia said with obvious concern in her voice.

"Not really, but at least Maria's got her steady job as a waitress. And you know I don't got nowhere else to go. And you know we love each other."

"I know that William, it's just that the two of you are so young. What do Maria's parents think of the idea?"

"To tell ya the truth I think they just want her out of the house too. If there was another way I'd do it but I can't think of nothin' else... can you?"

"To tell you the truth William, no I can't."

CHAPTER 20

Several weeks later things were looking up for William. For one, he had moved into a small one bedroom apartment on the lower east side of New Haven with Maria. Although their new home would be considered by most to be a 'rat trap' they were just happy to have a place of their own. Even the arguing neighbors and crying kids, whose voices pierced right through the thin walls, didn't seem to bother them. And two, Julia was able to get William a job as a cashier at the Yale Student Union Cafeteria. William was thrilled to have the job - any job, for that matter - but had a constant fear of getting fired. William had already made countless mistakes ringing up the food orders and he could tell his boss was getting agitated. On the other hand, Julia's university office was just a jaunt across the campus and William normally stopped by to say hello at the end of his day of work, and Julia, despite her busy schedule, was always happy to see him. Although she was desperately trying to keep her professional distance, Julia couldn't help but sincerely like William.

Julia had always wanted a family of her own, but circumstances always seemed to get in the way. First and foremost, Julia was a workaholic and didn't have much time to date, and when she wasn't working she was at home taking care of Mikey. Now Julia was forty-five and had basically resigned herself to the fact that she would never have kids of her own, although she always held on to a glimmer of hope. In a strange way William was becoming the surrogate son that Julia always wanted, and conversely, William thought of Julia as the type of mother that he had always wished for.

Julia found herself worrying about William more and more. *What would become of him?* And although Julia always tried to do her best without putting undue pressure on herself, she knew that it was up to her to save this young man she cared so deeply about.

CHAPTER 21

It was an overcast Friday afternoon. Julia, as usual, was busy in her lab. Her dry erase board was filled with notes, and vials of liquid and cages of animals cluttered the dark room. There was a knock on the door but Julia was so engrossed in her work that she didn't hear it. Another knock, this one a little louder, and it caught Julia's attention. "Come in."

William peered his head around the door. "Hi Dr. Pearlman," he said in a hushed tone.

"Hi William. Is everything alright?"

"Not really. I just got axed again."

"Oh William," Julia said, putting her hands to her head. "I'm so sorry. What happened?"

"The same shit as always," a disgusted William explained. "I just kept screwin' up and my boss told me he was sorry and all but it wasn't gonna work out. I just don't know what I'm gonna do now. Maria is counting on me to bring home my share of the rent and all."

"We'll figure something out," Julia said in as reassuring of a tone as she could muster. "Try not to worry too much and we'll discuss it tomorrow at our eight o'clock meeting… OK?"

"OK, I'll see you then." And with that William sulked out the door.

Julia quickly packed up the room. She knew that Stuart Sherman, the head of human services, normally worked late hours. Yet she also knew that it was Friday afternoon and that many Yale employees left early for their weekend plans. As Julia half walked and half jogged across the Yale campus she became wet with perspiration. As she entered the human services building she pushed the button for the elevator and wiped her brow. When she got to Stuart's office she was relieved to see him still at his desk. Stuart was a big man who was over six feet tall and weighed nearly three hundred pounds. He sported a fiery red go-tee that matched his hair. He was quite a menacing sight, but in reality Stuart was really a big teddy bear of a man who's soothing voice was more in liking to his personality.

"Hi Stu," Julia said as she stood in his doorway.

"Well, look who it is. Hello there stranger, long time no see. How have you been?"

"I'm doing well Stu, thanks for asking. How about yourself?"

"I'd complain but who'd listen?" Stu said with a laugh more to himself than out loud. "I had a feeling I might see you today."

"How's that?" Julia asked.

"I heard that things didn't work out too well for your friend we set up with a job a while back."

"Wow, good news really travels fast."

"It always does," Stu said with another laugh.

"Then I bet you can guess why I'm here."

"Before you get started Julia I can tell you that it's not the policy of the university to give recently fired employees another position."

"I realize that Stu, but I was hoping you might make an exception just this one time."

"I don't know Julia, it's really not the policy," Stu said, a sheepish look on his face.

"I would consider it a personal favor, Stu. Anything you can find. I'm sure he'll do anything. He's desperate."

Stu thought for a moment before saying, "How can I say no to you Julia? I'm sure we can find him something in the custodial department. Have him come to my office Monday morning and we'll give it another try."

"Thanks so much Stu. I really appreciate it." Julia left the office feeling relieved but knew that this fix was only temporary. Julia was certain that they would soon be back in the same position. Unfortunately, she was all too sure of it.

CHAPTER 22

Julia went to sleep that night worried again about William. She knew he would be excited about getting another job but also knew that a permanent fix needed to take place. Julia couldn't help but think of a proverb her father used to quote often: 'Feed a man a fish, he eats for a day. Teach a man to fish, he eats for a lifetime.' Up until now Julia felt like she was just feeding William one fish after another, and she knew that if she didn't teach him to fish for himself his problems would just continually follow him around.

As Julia lay in bed unable to sleep she looked at her alarm clock: it was one thirty in the morning. And then there was a loud BANG. Julia shot up from bed. *What the hell was that?* Julia ran to check on Mikey but found him sleeping soundly in his room. She smiled. Even though she knew what a deep sleeper her brother was even she didn't expect him to sleep through such a noise. Upon further inspection it became clear that the air conditioning had gone kaput. *There's nothing I can do about it now so I might as well go back to sleep,* she thought. Yet as the hours passed the heat of the night didn't make it any easier for her to sleep, and it didn't help that Julia and Mikey liked to sleep in an abnormally cool house, consequently keeping their house well colder than most.

As she tossed and turned she began to sweat. Early into the morning hours Julia felt as if she had just gotten out of the shower. At five o'clock she could fight the weather nor her mind no longer and finally got up to get some paperwork done. As she sat in her office sweating she began to think about her lab hamster, Sigmund. Although Siggy had made some progress the neurotransmitting agents she had been injecting him with just hadn't made the enormous difference she had hoped for. And then it hit her: the heat! It was made considerably worse by the contrast to her normally arctic house. Of course, while she had tried to raise the temperature of her whole concoction in the past she had only seen modest gain. However, by bringing the neurotransmitters up to an intensely hot temperature while simultaneously keeping the nonessential pharmaceutical agents significantly cooler there would surely be a heightened catalyst effect to help stimulate brain activity. Imagine the possibilities!

Although she was bursting at the seams she didn't want to go to her lab at such an early hour. Mikey was still sleeping and she had an appointment at eight o'clock with William. She would go directly after her session with William ended… she could hardly wait!

William showed up promptly at eight o'clock and Julia immediately gave him the good news about another chance at employment. "Thank you Dr. Pearlman. I don't know what I would do without you. I just hope I don't let you down again."

"Again? When have you let me down in the past?"

William shifted uncomfortably on the sofa. "It's just that I keep screwin' up and…" William paused, unsure as to whether he should finish his thought.

"Go ahead," Julia encouraged him. "You know you can tell me anything, and like I've promised you in the past, I'm not here to judge you but only to try and help."

William took a deep breath. "I just feel like if I keep messin' up you'll get sick of me just and drop me like a bad habit."

Julia was alarmed. She truly liked William and wanted desperately to help him, and she had no idea he felt so insecure with their relationship. "William, let me assure you that you will not be dropped. It's obvious to me that you're doing your best and being open and honest with me. That's all that I can ask for. Is that clear?"

"I guess so," William conceded.

"Good. Now I've got a favor to ask of you."

"Of me?" a shocked William responded. "How could I possibly help you?"

"Well something came up at work and I have to get to the lab. I was wondering, if you had the time, if you wouldn't mind spending some time with Mikey while I'm gone?"

"That's your big favor?" William said, wearing a sarcastic grin. "You know I like Mikey. It's no problem."

"Thank you William. I'll be back in a couple of hours. Are you sure you don't have any plans?"

"Anything for you, Dr. Pearlman."

And with that Julia was off to try and make history.

CHAPTER 23

As Julia made her way into the lab she was grateful for the solitude of a Saturday morning and for the modern technological advancements of air conditioning. She worked quickly yet methodically. She retrieved her most recent concoction of neurotransmitters from the cooler and nearly flew across her small lab to light the Bunsen burner. With the mixture heating she took Sigmund from his cage. *Poor Siggy,* she thought. *Another injection.* Julia had always had misgivings about animal research, but she felt that when it was truly for the betterment for mankind it was warranted.

She waited impatiently for the neurotransmitters to heat to four hundred degrees Fahrenheit. After carefully mixing the contrasting hot and freezing components of her drug she sucked up 10cc's of fluid into a syringe. She petted Siggy and rubbed his ear as she injected him in the back of the cortex. Siggy squirmed for a second, and it appeared as if his eyes glazed over, but after a few moments passed and Julia was convinced he was alright she put him back in his cage and began counting the minutes. It would take at least several weeks of daily injections for the drug to have its full effect. Julia would count the minutes to see if a lifetime of work had finally paid off.

CHAPTER 24

After several weeks of sleepless nights, this time due to anxiety now that the air conditioning had been fixed, Julia got out of bed early. After waiting as patiently as possible for Mikey to get ready to go to the YMCA for a day of activities she finally got him out the door and was off to the lab to check on Siggy.

As she approached his cage Julia noticed that her favorite pupil was running on his rotary wheel. She noted that this was something Sigmund rarely did. *Could this be a good sign?* she surmised. "I guess we'll find out soon enough won't we, Siggy?" she said out loud. Throughout her lab work Julia was constantly designing new structural mazes for her lab animals to run though. Her newest maze was purposely slightly harder than her previous creations.

Julia took Sigmund from his cage and grabbed her stopwatch. As she placed Sigmund at the starting position she said a prayer. *Please God, let my work be not in vain. Let my efforts and the gifts you have bestowed upon me work together for the betterment of mankind.* As she pulled up the starting shoot and pressed the start button on her stopwatch she watched in amazement as Sigmund quickly maneuvered his way through the maze. "Oh my God," she said aloud. "It's working… it's really working!"

As Sigmund finished the maze Julia entered his time into her computer. She had déjà vu as she waited for the results to come back. And then it happened. *This subject has completed his assignment 84% faster than all other subjects recorded.*

Julia just sat and stared at the computer screen with tears rolling down her face. She had done it. Finally, after years of schooling, research and hard work, she had done it. A medication that would potentially help all of those struggling with learning difficulties around the globe. Julia could hardly believe it.

CHAPTER 25

For the next several weeks Julia threw herself into her work, spending every possible moment in the lab monitoring Sigmund's every move. After obtaining enough new data to fill her three-ring binder Julia was ready to take the next step and share her findings with her colleagues. Julia's memo to the psychiatry faculty at Yale was purposely vague. She sent out an email simply stating: "I will be presenting some recent research findings in the west conference hall of the graduate faculty building tomorrow at two o'clock. Your presence will be much appreciated. – Julia." She knew that such an impromptu meeting would be sure to raise some eyebrows, but now that her research was clear she could barely contain her enthusiasm. Even though she couldn't wait to share her findings with her fellow academicians she took an almost devilish pleasure in keeping them in the dark for now. She could hardly wait to see the expressions on their collective faces when she sprung what would be one of the most important psychological discoveries in the prestigious university's history.

In preparation for the big presentation Julia cancelled all of her classes and office hours for the preceding day. After locking herself in her office Julia got to work like only she could, and nearly twelve hours later she finally came up for air. Lecture notes were written and rewritten. Slides were prepared. Posters were drawn up and laminated. Although she was exhausted and starving she could hardly suppress a smile as she walked across campus and got into her nearly ten-year-old dark blue Saab.

That night Julia lay in bed, her mind racing. How would her lifetime of research be received? Would it be with the handshakes and hugs of sincere congratulations? Or was there an obvious flaw in her findings that she had failed to see? "Impossible," Julia whispered to herself. "I've gone over these results countless times. There's no way I could have missed anything." Yet as midnight turned into one o'clock, and one o'clock turned to two, and then to three her mind nor her paranoia would let her sleep. Finally, at three thirty in the morning she could fight her subconscious no longer, and got up to review her research for the umpteenth time.

As Julia lay on her office black leather sofa her mind would not let up. Two o'clock couldn't come quickly enough. And yet as she curled her legs up into a fetal position she could feel herself reverting into a Freudian childhood existence. *What if I've made a mistake?* she began to worry. *Impossible,* she reassured herself again. *But what if...?* And suddenly, as the 'what if' game began to consume her, she felt herself beginning to hope that two o'clock would never come at all.

CHAPTER 26

As the clock moved interminably slowly Julia could not concentrate on anything but her upcoming lecture. Incredibly, for the first time in her fifteen years at Yale, Julia cancelled classes on back to back days. But finally, mercifully, the fateful hour came to fruition, and the mahogany conference hall began to fill with a handful of the brightest psychological minds in the world. Although Julia could not have been more prepared she wanted to crawl and hide behind the podium where she stood. The last of the faculty made their way into their seats, and now the time of judgment stood imminently before her. As she took a deep breath she actually began to feel slightly faint. As she usually did in this type of situation, Julia used her brother's image to steady her. She felt her feet firm up beneath her, then began with an almost unperceivable crack in her voice.

"First of all I want to thank you all for coming on such short notice. I know how busy you all are, but I have some research to share with you that I hope you will find as exciting as I do. As most of you know, I have been trying my entire professional career to make a breakthrough in the realm of learning disabilities. As I have discussed with many of you in the past, I've always felt that with the right combination of neurotransmitting agents a medication could be created that would someday conceivably help the millions of LD sufferers around the world." And now it was time to drop the bombshell. She took a deep breath. "Well ladies and gentlemen, I stand humbly before you, my distinguished colleagues, to say that I believe today is that day!" A loud murmur broke out through the conference room. Julia plowed ahead. "Now I'm sure that many of you have questions, but I believe that my presentation will answer most of them."

Julia spent the next three hours painstakingly explaining every aspect of her research, even mentioning the fortuitous act of the air-conditioning breaking.

"Remember, although this is the product of a lifetime of research, the latest findings are only weeks old. Consequently, it will most likely be years before any of this comes to fruition. I would like to thank you all for attending, and would now like to open the floor to questions," she concluded. As she looked out into the eyes of her respected peers her heart began to race. The room was filled with silence. For what felt like an eternity no one said a word. It was her worst fear. *There must have been an obvious flaw,* she thought, panicking. Another moment passed with more silence. Julia wanted to cry. And then it happened - a *crack*.

What the hell was that? Julia nearly blurted out. And then another *crack*, but this time it was apparent. As the group of onlookers began a resounding roar of clapping they stood to their feet, giving Julia a well deserved standing ovation. Julia beamed - she had done it. She had reached the pinnacle of her career, but more importantly, she knew she had fulfilled her destiny by creating a drug that would help countless others who were less fortunate then her. She knew her parents were looking down on her proudly. And with that the handshakes and hugs that she had dreamt about merely hours ago became a reality.

CHAPTER 27

While things couldn't be going better for Julia, they couldn't be worse for William. After working as a custodian at the university for just a couple of weeks he had already been reprimanded several times. And to make things worse, William's problems at work were starting to put a strain on his relationship with Maria. Although Maria was always supportive of William and his trials and tribulations with work, the economic realities of living on their own were obviously affecting her. As William began to lament on his most recent tongue lashing, Maria had had enough. "Will!" she exclaimed, "I just can't take it anymore. You know I love you, but we just can't keep going on this way. I barely make enough with my pathetic job to pay half of the rent, and if you get fired again we're in big trouble. Our landlord has already told us that he won't tolerate another late rent payment. I'm at my wits end. You just can't get fired again."

"Is that some kind of a threat?" a now defensive William

countered.

"It's not a threat Will, it's just reality. If you lose this job I'm going to have to move back in with my parents."

"Damn it Maria, where the hell is this coming from all of the sudden? You know I'm trying my best."

"I know Will, but it's not all of the sudden. It's been a long time coming." William knew deep down that Maria was as loyal as they come, but his feelings of abandonment that began with his father and continued throughout his life suddenly came rushing to the surface. William's heart began to race and his face turned beet red.

"Well let me tell you something, Maria," William stammered. "What you see is what you get. I'm doing my best, and if this idiot isn't good enough for you then the hell with it. And for that matter, the hell with you!"

As William made his way toward the door Maria broke down in tears. "Please Willy, don't go. I'm sorry... can't we talk about it?" she pleaded.

"I think you've done enough talking for the both of us!"

"At least tell me where you're going, it's getting late."

"I don't know where I'm going and I don't know when I'll be back, but I do know one thing - I've got to get the hell out of here!"

And with that William slammed the door behind him to the sound of Maria's tears.

As night turned into early morning William had yet to return. Maria, who was overwhelmed with fear, didn't know where to turn. Finally, out of desperation, she called Julia. When the phone rang at five o'clock it was rarely a good thing. The ringing phone startled Julia, who nearly jumped out of bed. "Hello?" she answered hoarsely.

The voice on the other end of the line immediately put Julia even more on edge - it was weak and filled with fear. "Hello Dr. Pearlman, it's Maria Rinaldi... William Victory's girlfriend," she whimpered. "I'm sorry to call you so early but I just don't know what to do... I'm so scared."

"It's OK Maria. Take a deep breath and tell me what's going on."

Although Julia was obviously concerned her voice had an air of confidence that put Maria at ease. "It's just that me and Will had this big fight last night and he still hasn't come home. I'm so worried, Dr. Pearlman."

"It's alright Maria. You did the right thing by calling me. I'm sure he's fine, but let's see if we can put our heads together and figure out where he might be. Just take your time and tell me what happened."

As Maria recalled the events of the previous evening Julia's mind raced. Although she always fought to keep her clinical judgment with patients, William was clearly special. As Julia forced herself to remain objective she listened intently. When Maria finished recanting the night's events Julia asked the obvious question. "So Maria, do you have any idea where he could be?"

"Absolutely none, Dr. Pearlman. That's what's got me so worried."

"Well I'm sure everything is fine, but just as a precaution I think it would be prudent to call the police and local hospitals."

While Julia and Maria were dividing the phone calls between them there was a faint knock at the door. Then again, this time a little bit louder. Julia asked Maria to hold for a moment as she rushed to the door. As she peered through the peep hole she felt a sense of enormous relief, then she flung the door open.

"William!" Julia nearly screamed through a whisper so as not to wake Mikey. "We've been worried sick about you. Are you alright?"

"What do you mean, we?" an exhausted and puffy-eyed William inquired.

"Maria called me extremely worried and... oh my gosh, I forgot she was still on the phone."

"Maria's on the phone?" an embarrassed William asked. "Why did she have to call you?"

"I'll explain everything in a minute. Please just come in and sit down." William walked through the foyer and made his way into Julia's office, then plopped down on the sofa as he listened to Julia pass on the news to Maria. "Yes Maria, he's here... yes he's fine. Wait a minute, let me check. Maria wants to know if she can talk to you, William." As William slowly shook his head from side to side Julia returned her attention to Maria. "Why don't you let me talk to him for a few minutes first honey, and then I'm sure he'll contact you soon. But please try not to worry... he seems fine."

As Julia hung up the phone she looked to William. She knew this was a delicate moment and she would have to handle it just so, but before she could speak William beat her to the punch. "Dr. Pearlman, I'm sorry to bother you in this mess and barge in on you so early, but I'm really not up for talking right now. I just need a place to sleep. I know it's a lot to ask for, but if I could just sleep on your sofa for a few hours I promise to get out of your hair."

Julia responded with concern and affection in her voice.

"William, first of all you can stay here as long as you like. And second of all, I don't want you out of my hair. Not now, not tomorrow, not ever. Just promise me that after you get some rest you'll talk this thing out with Maria and me."

"I guess I can do that," William reluctantly agreed. And with that William lay down and quickly fell asleep.

When William awoke several hours later Julia listened intently as he painstakingly detailed the prior day's altercation with Maria. "I guess I just can't take someone who's not loyal. That's all there is to it," William summed up.

"But William," Julia rebutted, "You've always said that Maria is the only person in your life that's always been there for you. The only person that you feel totally comfortable with. The only person with whom you can completely be yourself without reservation."

"That all may have been true in the past Dr. Pearlman, but now I'm not so sure. I mean if she can't support me when times get tough then maybe she ain't as loyal as I thought she was."

Julia spent the rest of their session patiently detailing all of Maria's finer qualities. Due to Julia's persuasiveness, as well as William's great respect for her opinion, he begrudgingly acquiesced to give Maria another chance. But Julia knew that their relationship was now tenuous, to say the least. Since she had first met William, Julia knew that he would require tremendous support. At this current point in time William could rely on Julia to some degree, but most importantly he had Maria. Without Maria's consistent love and encouragement William was like a ship without a compass. Now Julia shuddered at the very real possibility that in the very near future she would be the only thing between William and his ship being completely lost at sea.

CHAPTER 28

When Julia woke up the following morning she had mixed emotions. She was almost euphoric with the knowledge of where her latest discovery might take her but also felt simultaneously guilty about being so happy. She marveled at the fact that things could be going so well in her life while William was struggling so mightily. Yet she reconciled her inner turmoil with the belief that her work would directly impact William, and the thousands of others like him. Yet she was also all too well aware that even if her lifetime of work continued to move forward with the momentum of a locomotive it would still be years before the learning disabled society would see the benefits of her tears and sweat. It took large pharmaceutical companies years to push their drugs through FDA approval, and she knew all too well that even with the backing of a prestigious university like Yale it would be a monumental effort to get her drug to the public in an expeditious fashion. Would it be too late to help William? Julia would do everything in her power to make sure that William didn't fall through the cracks. This was a vow she would take seriously… VERY seriously.

CHAPTER 29

Julia returned to her lab at Yale with a jaunt in her step. Before her drug had the chance of becoming a reality there would be months of research and testing, and then it still had to be approved by an FDA bureaucrat. Julia unlocked her door, hung up her jacket, and as usual went to check her messages. But this was not a usual Monday morning, and when Julia looked closely at her blinking answering machine she was in shock.

"Twenty-two messages?" she questioned out loud. "Can that be right?" But when Julia pushed the play button her shock turned to anger as she listened to what would be the first of a barrage of reporters soliciting her for an interview.

"Uh hello Dr. Pearlman, my name is Jordan Pinsky and I'm a reporter calling from the Washington Post. Congratulations on your discovery. I'd love to meet with you for an interview at your convenience. Please give me a call at (781) 555-1287 and my secretary will set something up. Cheers… click." This message was followed by calls from reporters from all across the country, and by the time Julia had gotten halfway through them she had had enough. Now fuming, she immediately picked up the phone then slammed it back down. No, she would do this in person.

In no mood to wait for the elevator, she made her way to the stairs and raced up three flights. She proceeded to jog down the long corridor, pushing her way through the door to the corner office. "Good morning Dr. Pearlman," said the smiling secretary, but Julia was in no mood for pleasantries. As she continued to walk toward the department chair's office a now concerned secretary tried to stop her. "He's on an important phone call, Dr. Pearlman. Please have a seat and I'll let him know you're here."

But Julia would not be deterred, and she flung the door open to see a shocked Dr. Angelo Campanella on the phone. He held up his hand in an attempt to finish his call, but Julia shot into her tirade immediately.

"Angelo, this can't wait." Angelo Campanella was a man with a distinguished reputation who commanded respect, and while he would normally be annoyed by such a blatantly rude act he knew that this must be important if it came from the typically reserved Julia.

"I'll have to call you back Roger," he uttered and hung up the phone. "What is it, Julia? What's got you so full of venom this morning?" Julia, who was now whirling at windmills, was ready to lash out.

"How could this happen, Ang?"

"How could what happen?" a concerned department chair inquired.

"There's been a leak!"

"What kind of leak? Did one of the pipes break in your office?"

"No Angelo, a leak of information. I had over twenty messages on my machine this morning from reporters asking for information on my latest research findings. And as we are all too well aware, all of my findings are still confidential, so I'm wondering how in the world this could have happened?"

Now Angelo was perturbed as well. "First of all Julia, let me tell you I'm sorry. This has yet to happen under my watch, and it will be dealt with severely. I guess, however, we shouldn't be completely surprised."

"What do you mean, Angelo?"

"Well a discovery this big hasn't come along in decades, Julia. I guess it was just too tantalizing for someone to hold to themselves."

"Well that's just great, Angelo. It's not enough that I have a lifetime of research at stake, but now I'm going to have to deal with reporters from here to Kalamazoo. How am I supposed to get any work done?" This question was followed by silence as Angelo and Julia both pondered this most recent dilemma.

Angelo spoke first. "I think I've got the answer. We should call a press conference."

"A press conference?" Julia countered. "But that will take time to arrange and will most likely turn into a circus."

"That may be true Julia, but think of the alternative. If you try and answer the reporters one by one you'll be on the phone for weeks."

"What if I just ignore them?" Julia proposed.

"Not a chance," Angelo chuckled. "These reporters are like pit bulls when they think they've got a juicy tidbit. And believe me Julia, they don't come any juicier than this. No, the best course of action will be to bite the bullet and get it over with all at once. It won't be pleasant but at least it will clear off your plate and you can get back to work."

Julia though for a moment before responding. "I guess you're right, Ang... but all those people? I nearly passed out while giving the presentation in front of my peers. How will I do it?"

"I don't know Julia but you'd better get used to it, because like it or not this thing has the potential to put you in the spotlight for the rest of your life!"

Julia let her esteemed colleagues words set in for a minute, and as the realization of what she had embarked upon began to seemingly unfold before her she took a deep breath and swallowed. "Oh my God," she said more to herself than to Angelo. "What have I done?"

CHAPTER 30

With the help of Dr. Campanella, as well as the information division's administration office, a large press conference was scheduled for two days later. Yet this time, due to the buzz that was starting to take place literally around the country, it would take place in the largest auditorium on campus. And to Julia's dismay, it was standing room only.

As Julia prepared herself for what she considered to be an overwhelming experience her knees were literally knocking. Dr. Campanella, who was to introduce Julia, could sense her apprehension. He approached her behind the closed, large velvet curtain that enveloped the stage. "Julia," he began, "are you alright? You look a little flushed."

Julia could feel the blood draining out of her face. "I'm just a little nervous, Ang. I mean, did you see all those people?"

"If it makes you feel any better Julia I'm pretty nervous myself, and I'm just introducing you," Angelo said through a subtle smile.

"But I guess there's no time like the present."

"Do we have to?" Julia joked. "There's still time to make a break for it." They both let out some nervous laughter and the tension was released, if just for a moment.

"You'll be fine, Julia. Just remember, keep it simple. Most of these people are not scientists. They are simply lay people trying to understand what it is you've accomplished. And trust me, if you get too technical it will just lead to more questions. Capisci?"

"Yeah, I got it. Thanks for the advice." And with that Angelo slipped through the curtain and onto the stage as the audience quieted down to a murmur. Angelo tapped on the microphone to make sure it was working, and was then ready to address the largest audience he had stood in front of in years.

"Ladies and gentleman, first of all I want to thank you all for coming for such an auspicious occasion. My name is Dr. Angelo Campanella, and I am the chair of the psychiatry department here at Yale. I am standing before you today to introduce a woman with whom I have worked for over a decade. Dr. Julia Pearlman earned her Bachelor of Science degree from Dartmouth college and obtained her medical and Ph.D. degrees from Harvard University. She has been a distinguished professor and researcher at Yale for fifteen years. Through her years of dedicated effort I believe that she has made a breakthrough the likes of which has not been seen for years. We here at Yale are extremely privileged to work with Dr. Pearlman, and I am proud to call her my colleague and, more importantly, my friend. I realize that you all did not come here today to here an old fogy like me speak, so without further ado I give you Dr. Julia Pearlman." As the crowd broke into a polite yet semi-excited applause Julia's heart raced and she felt a lump in her throat. As she stood in front of the podium and looked out at the multitude of faces she actually felt a little nauseous. Yet, as she always did in these situations, she visualized her brother's face. Julia had to marvel at how well she was able to calm herself under such nerve-racking conditions.

Although Julia had thoroughly prepared a well-thought out presentation, she decided to take Angelo's advice and simple it down. The last thing she wanted was to finish her speech only to have to answer a barrage of questions. As she began to speak in front of this large audience she was surprised to find herself so composed. And incredibly, as the hour long presentation passed, she was actually beginning to enjoy herself. When she was wrapping up she had an inner contentment - she knew she had achieved her objective. She ended by taking a deep breath and soliciting, "Now if there are any questions I'd be happy to try and answer them."

To Julia's shock and dismay a multitude of questions shot through the air. "Please," Julia pleaded, "one at a time." A man with a booming voice grabbed command and fired off the first question.

"Dr. Pearlman, is it true that the new drug can increase one's I.Q. by one hundred points or more?" Julia was flabbergasted. Where in the world did he come up with that? Wasn't he listening to the presentation at all?

"No, that's not accurate," Julia answered, as politely as she could. "As I stated earlier, in simple terms this drug was specifically designed to alleviate the faulty wiring that occurs in a distinct portion of the population. Consequently, it will only be effective for those with learning disabilities." Unfortunately, this answer was followed by an onslaught of bizarre questions the likes of which Julia couldn't imagine. As she attempted to fend them off one at a time she began to feel overwhelmed.

Thankfully, after approximately forty-five minutes of agony,

Angelo sensed her apprehension and came to her aid. He shimmied up beside Julia and raised both hands to the crowd. "Ladies and gentleman, I want to thank you all for coming today. Unfortunately, do to time constraints we'll have to wrap up the presentation at this time. Please direct all further questions to the information center at the university. Thank you again, and I bid you all a good day." Before Julia knew what had hit her she was mercifully being whisked off the stage to a bombardment of further questions. When they got backstage a frazzled Julia turned to Angelo.

"What the hell just happened out there? Those people were acting like wolves, and I was the sheep."

"I don't know Julia, but I'm afraid this is just the beginning."

And with this realization they both scurried back to their respective offices, wholly afraid of what was yet to come.

CHAPTER 31

Due to Julia's newfound fame she had to change her phone numbers and lurk around in the shadows of New Haven in an attempt to remain anonymous. Although her life was in a tail spin she tried to keep grounded by reminding herself that she was on the verge of creating a breakthrough that was a lifetime in the making. In an effort to meet the demanding pressures that were now upon her she had to make some sacrifices. She cut back on her office hours, was planning on reducing her teaching classes by fifty percent for the upcoming semester, and had referred all of her personal patients to other therapists - with the exception of William. That was one sacrifice she would not make. She made a resolution that no matter what else happened she would do everything in her power to help William.

As William sat in Julia's office on a rainy Saturday morning he was unusually quiet, and Julia wondered why. "William," she began, "is everything alright?"

"I guess so. Why?" he more grunted than asked.

"It's just that you seem so quiet. I know things have been tough recently but you appear unusually despondent today. Is there anything I should know about?" William sat silently for a couple of seconds, apparently debating whether or not to spill what was on his mind. "Go ahead, William," Julia prodded "You know you can tell me anything."

"Well Dr. Pearlman, I've been hearin' all about your recent discovery on TV, and I'm real happy for you and all, but…"

"Please William, say what's on your mind."

William raised his head and looked directly into Julia's caring eyes, and he knew once again that he could tell her anything. "It's just that I'm afraid you're gonna get too busy for me. I mean, you've already cancelled on two of our sessions. And believe me, I know how busy you are, but I'm just afraid…"

Julia cut him off instantly. "William, I'm sorry I've been so busy, but I promise I will not cut you out of my life. I probably shouldn't be telling you this in session but Mikey and I consider you like family. I will do anything I can to help you. Do you understand that, William? I consider you like family." William did not respond but simply looked down at the floor. "William, do you understand what I'm saying?" As William looked up Julia could see that his eyes were full with tears.

"Yeah, I understand Dr. Pearlman," he choked out. "And you'll never know how much that means to me."

But Julia did know. To a young man as vulnerable as William it meant everything. Julia was all too well aware that her relationship with William was now permanent, and she couldn't be happier about it.

CHAPTER 32

As Julia continued on her whirlwind journey things were simultaneously incredibly chaotic and crystal clear. With reporters and pharmaceutical companies bombarding her with mail, ringing her phone off the hook (despite the fact that her number was now unlisted), and literally stalking her on campus and at her home, Julia was steadied by the fact that her drug was steadily moving in the right direction. It seemed like her progress was making leaps and bounds on an almost daily basis. Yet with all of her newfound successes Julia was torn. Sure she could put up with all of the insanity following her progress, but all of her time at work was severely cutting into her obligations with Mikey and William. Although these two men constantly reassured her that they understood how busy she was she knew how desperately they both needed her in their respective lives. And while she knew that her work was for the betterment of mankind she was still guilt ridden.

Julia finally made the tough decision that she wouldn't let her work take precedence over her personal obligations. But there had to be a happy medium. There had to be some way to have her cake and eat it too... but how? After mulling over this quandary for some time she hadn't made any progress. At her wits end, Julia decided to just be honest with the two men in her life and see if they could put their three heads together to come up with a solution.

As Julia met with William on their weekly Saturday morning session she planned on sharing her dilemma with him. When he walked into her office she blurted out, "William, I need to ask you something." But before he could answer Julia saw what was written all over his face - a look that she had come to know and dread.

Before William could reply Julia cut him off. "Did it happen again, William?"

"Yeah. How'd you know?" William nearly whispered.

"I just had a hunch. Do you mind telling me what happened?" Julia stated sympathetically.

"It's the same story. I kept screwin' up. My boss said he was sorry and all but he had no choice but to give me the ax. If I can't even keep a job as a freakin' janitor how am I gonna make ends meet?" Silence filled the room as William and Julia both pondered the gravity of this question.

William finally broke the silence. "And I don't know how I'm going to tell Maria. You remember what happened the last time. I'm afraid she'll dump me for sure." As the patient and therapist spent the rest of the session mulling over possible scenarios Julia finally came to the only viable solution.

"William, I don't think there's any way around it. You have to be honest with Maria and let the chips fall where they may. She's going to find out eventually."

"I know," William said, defeated. "I just wish there was some other way."

"So do I," Julia sympathized, "So do I."

As William began to walk out of Julia's office he turned back, suddenly remembering something. "Wasn't there somethin' you wanted to ask me?"

But at this point Julia couldn't bear to put anything more on William's wilting shoulders. "You know what William, it really wasn't that important. It can wait." And with that William went off to face the love of his life for what he hoped wouldn't be a final conversation.

CHAPTER 33

William walked home slowly. As he listlessly made his way through the slum-filled streets of his neighborhood he tried to run the multitude of possible scenarios with Maria through his head. But as William finally made his way to his apartment building he realized that he was just going to have to wing it and, as Julia said, 'let the chips fall where they may.' As William walked through the front door his heart immediately sank. There was Maria, his beloved, sitting at the pink formica table they had purchased at a garage sale with tears in her eyes. How had she found out, William wondered. Was it possible that Dr. Pearlman had called her? *Impossible... Dr. Pearlman would never break my confidence. But then how did Maria find out?*

William decided to beat Maria to the punch. "Maria, don't cry. I know things are rough, but I promise you I'll find another job. I'll start looking tomorrow," William pleaded.

"What are you talking about, Will? Oh my God. Please don't

tell me you got fired again. Please don't tell me that, Will," Maria nearly wailed.

"I thought you knew," William stated as he sat down next to her. "If it's not my job then what is it... what going on?"

"I've got some bad news Will. I mean, really bad news."

"What the hell is it? Please Maria, tell me!" William nearly shouted, anxiety surging through his veins.

"I'm pregnant Will!" Maria shouted back. "I'm pregnant!"

CHAPTER 34

William and Maria spent the first of what would be many sleepless nights to come together. Although William was technically Catholic he couldn't remember the last time he had been to church, and in reality he wondered if he even believed in a supreme being anymore. *If there is a God why would he give me such a terrible life?* William surmised. Maria was Catholic as well, but unlike William she was quite religious and even attended church regularly. Consequently, as far as she was concerned an abortion was out of the question. There was no doubt about it, Maria was going to have this baby.

To William's credit he was wholly supportive of Maria's decision. As nervous as he was about being a father and all of the responsibilities that went along with it, he was going to support Maria. The last thing he was going to be was an absentee parent like that bastard father of his. He had long ago made a vow that if he were ever to have children he would damn well make sure that he was the complete opposite of that good for nothing sperm donor that gave rise to his own miserable existence.

After a night full of talking and crying William made a decision that at first surprised even himself, but after a few moments he knew what he had to do. He turned toward Maria as the dawn began to break, his heart and mind racing.

"Maria, I think we should get married," he said. Maria just lay there without moving a muscle. "Maria, did you hear what I said?"

"Yeah I heard you Will, but are you sure? I mean, it's just that we're so young…"

William sat up in bed. "If we're gonna have a baby together then I think it's the right thing to do… don't you?"

In actuality Maria was terrified of having this baby by herself, and if there was one thing she knew it was that she loved Will. Sure they were young, but who's to say that they couldn't get married? People do it all the time. The more Maria thought about the more it made sense.

"Yes William, I do think it's the right thing to do," Maria said, a small smile starting to penetrate the corners of her mouth. William jumped out of bed and began pacing back and forth.

"Are we really gonna do this?" he asked expectantly.

"I think so!" she answered excitedly. A moment passed. And then another. Then William walked over to Maria's side of the bed and got down on one knee. With both of their eyes now full of tears, William cleared his throat.

"Maria Louise Rinaldi… will you marry me?"

"You better believe it!" Maria exclaimed as she jumped out of bed and threw her arms around him. "I love you, William," she whispered into his ear.

"I love you too," he whispered back.

CHAPTER 35

It had been six months since Julia made her breakthrough, and during that time things had progressed quite rapidly. Due to her incredible work ethic and the support of the entire faculty at Yale, Julia was ready to take the next step. She sent a mass email to the entire psychiatry faculty asking them to meet her and review her most recent findings in one week's time. With the buzz and excitement surrounding the project she knew that no one would miss it.

As the day arrived Julia was, as always, thoroughly prepared. With the faculty hanging on every word she meticulously laid out her most up-to-date research. Throughout her presentation she was bolstered by the nods of approval from around the room. At one point, as she described a particularly riveting piece of information, she actually heard one of her colleagues say "wow" before catching himself and regaining his professional composure.

As her presentation came to an end Julia looked expectantly at her compatriots. "Well... what do you think? Is this project ready for the next step? Are we ready to go for FDA approval?" she asked, holding her breath. As the faculty looked around the room, waiting for someone to make the first gesture, it was Angelo Campanella who finally broke the silence. As Angelo stood up he cleared his throat.

"Julia, you've done some amazing work here, and more importantly, you have the findings to back it up. I know it may seem quick to some, but I think applying for FDA approval is more than warranted at this point."

"Hear-hear," came the flock of approval from the remaining staff.

As the faculty began to shuffle up their papers and exit the room they all made sure to congratulate Julia one more time. As Julia modestly accepted the well wishes of her colleagues she was literally beaming. The room finally cleared out, and only Julia and Angelo were left. He approached Julia and extended his hand.

"Congratulations, Julia. You should really be proud of yourself," Angelo stated sincerely.

"You know what Ang, I really am."

"And you should be. Now I don't want to burst your bubble, but this is the first time in your career that you've attempted to gain FDA approval is it not?"

"That's right, Angelo. As you know I've basically spent my whole career on this one endeavor and consequently haven't had the thrill, but I hear it can be a difficult process."

Angelo gave a knowing nod of the head. "Difficult to say the least. These FDA bureaucrats can really be ball-busters, Julia. Please excuse my language, but I've been around the block several times with them in the past and it can be years of arduous work only to be rejected and sent back to the drawing board. I just want you to be aware of what you're in for."

And all of a sudden it hit Julia like a ton of bricks. This wasn't the end of a lifetime of work... this was just the beginning. Immediately Julia thought of Mikey and William. There wasn't enough time in the day as it was and now this was sure to double her work load.

As the blood drained from Julia's face she went pale. "Are you alright Julia?" a concerned Angelo inquired. "You don't look well."

"I'm not sure," Julia managed to squeak out. "I'm just not sure."

CHAPTER 36

Not one to waste any time, Julia jumped right into the FDA approval process. On a clear, crisp Saturday morning Julia was at her desk at six o'clock. With a little help from Angelo Julia acquired the necessary forms and had them strewn across her desk. This was only the first step in the approval process and Julia was already overwhelmed. But as was her style Julia threw herself into the work, and by the time she looked up at the clock it was already eight forty-five.

What happened to the time? Julia wondered. She paused for a minute to catch her breath and suddenly it hit her - where's William? He was supposed to be there at eight o'clock. As she continued to clear her head from an FDA-induced fog she could barely make out a conversation from what sounded like the living room. She stood up out of her black leather chair and slowly opened the door to her office. As she peered around the corner she saw a scene that did her heart good - William and Mikey were playing chutes and ladders and having a full-fledged conversation. She watched for several minutes, a smile slowly crossing her face. She finally approached the two men.

"You two look like you're having a good time," she stated, a smile in her voice.

"Oh hi Julie," Mikey answered. "William and me are playing," he said gleefully.

"I can see that. How long have you been here William?" Julia inquired.

"I got here at eight and Mikey let me in. When I saw your door was shut I figured you were busy so Mikey and I were just hanging out until you were ready. I hope that's OK?"

"That's terrific. I actually really appreciate it. But I am sorry to have kept you waiting, I completely lost track of the time," Julia apologized.

"No problem. We were having a good time, right Mikey?"

"Right!" Mikey said through a wide grin.

"Well boys, I hate to break up this little pow-wow but if it's OK I'd like to talk to William for a little while now."

"Does he have to go Julie?" Mikey whined.

"I'll tell you what, Mikey," William said. "If it's OK with Dr. Pearlman we'll spend some time together after I meet with her."

"Can he Julie, can he?" Mikey pleaded.

"If he's got the time I don't see why not. But for now I need to talk to William privately."

William and Julia made their way back to Julia's office and took their respective seats on the chair and sofa. As the therapist and patient began their session Julia's head was still spinning from her FDA paperwork, but after a few minutes of talking with William she had a full-fledged migraine.

"Maria's pregnant?! ... You're getting married?!" Julia could hardly believe it. She had had her reservations when the young couple initially moved in together, but now her fears had become a reality. "Are you sure you're ready for all of this William?" Julia asked worriedly.

"It's not a matter of being ready. I've got to do what I've got to do," William answered maturely. And in actuality William was quite mature for his age. Sure he had a lot to learn about the world but his tough upbringing had forced him to grow up quickly, and Julia took resolve in this fact.

"Well," Julia began, "it sounds like you've thought this out. But I hope both you and Maria are aware of the perils of being young, newly married, and first time parents."

"We are," William tried to answer confidently, even though he was as frightened as could be. "It's just that I can't keep a job. How am I going to support a family if I can't even hold on to a stupid job?" As Julia pondered the question the session was coming to an end. "Let's both think about it a little bit more. I'm sure we'll think of something," Julia said reassuringly. "Now are you sure you have time to spend with Mikey? The last thing I want to do is impose on your time."

"What else do I have to do?" William said. "It's not like I've got a job to go to, and Maria's at work. Plus, you know I like hanging out with Mikey."

"Thank you William. I really appreciate your help. I'll be in my office working if you need me."

"We'll be fine, Dr. Pearlman." As William went to the living room to play with Mikey Julia made her way back to her desk, and faced a mountain of paperwork. All of the sudden the magnitude of the work facing her hit her again like a ton of bricks. *How am I going to get all of this accomplished and still have time for my life?* she thought for the hundredth time. And then the light bulb went off. *Of course,* she mouthed, *why hadn't I thought about this sooner?*

Julia nearly jumped out of her seat and made her way to the living room. "Mikey, William, I'm sorry to bother you again but I have an important question for the two of you." As the two friends looked at Julia expectantly she continued. "I think I've found a temporary solution to our problems. William, you obviously need a job. Mikey, you need someone to spend more time with you. And I need a little more time to get my work done, so…Tadaa," Julia announced, a lilt in her voice. "What would you say, William, if I offered you a job to look after Mikey during the afternoons when he comes home from work? I can't pay you that much, but until you find something permanent it might be a temporary fix. What do you say? Would that work for both of you?" But she didn't need a verbal answer - her question was answered by the smiling faces of the two participants in question. "I take it that's a yes?"

"That's a definite yes for me, Dr. Pearlman," William answered.

"Me too, Julie," Mikey said, delighted.

"Terrific!" Julia said as she breathed a sigh of relief.

CHAPTER 37

Like many women, Maria had always dreamed of a big wedding in a beautiful church surrounded by lots of friends and family. However, with no money, few friends, a disapproving family and the realities of a shot-gun wedding, Maria and William resigned themselves to the fact that eloping made the most sense. And inexplicitly, a little over a week after they found out they were pregnant, William and Maria found themselves in the New Haven courthouse in the judge's chambers.

The honorable Robert L. Dragunoff was a formidable presence, although you wouldn't know it by looking at him. Standing at five feet four inches tall (with his thick soles on), he weighed in at a minuscule one hundred and twenty pounds. His steely eyes and booming voice made him an apparent force to be reckoned with, but everyone who really knew him understood that Judge Dragunoff was really a pussy cat on the inside. Yes, he could be tough when he had to be, and he didn't blink while serving life sentences to the dreads of society, but in actuality this was his favorite part of the job.

Judge Dragunoff loved weddings. And with William and Maria on this very special day were their best man and maid of honor... Mikey and Julia. As the ensemble gathered in front of the judge everyone looked beautiful. Judge Dragunoff, William and Mikey all wore suits (it was Williams only suit), while Julia wore her second favorite dress. Her favorite dress just happened to be white, and was being adorned by Maria. As the judge stood before the wedding party everyone's collective minds were racing. But as Judge Dragnuoff's baritone voice enveloped the room all were brought back to the present.

"Dearly beloved, we are brought together on this day, Sunday, the 24th of June, for the wedding of William Nathan Victory and Maria Louise Rinaldi. A wedding is a culmination of two world's full of love, and we are all blessed to be witness to such a joyful event. After speaking with William and Maria, it is evident to me that they care very deeply for one another and are very much in love. Therefore, it is my distinct honor and pleasure to officiate over such a blessed union. However, a wedding should never be entered into without much thought and introspection. Consequently, if anyone should have hesitation as to why this man and this woman should not marry, let them speak now or forever hold their peace." While everyone in the room felt more than a little hesitation no one dared to speak. William even made eye contact with Julia just to make sure, but when she nodded her head approvingly William knew that they were clear for takeoff.

After the moment passed Judge Dragunoff continued. "Do you, William Nathan Victory, take this woman to be your lawfully wedded wife, to love and to honor, to have in sickness and in health, till death do you part?" William looked right into Maria's beautiful green eyes and instantly knew that he was doing the right thing.

"I do." As William placed the gold wedding band (a gift from Julia) on Maria's finger, Judge Dragunoff turned toward the bride.

"And do you, Maria Louise Rinaldi, take this man to be your lawfully wedded husband, to love and to honor, to have in sickness and in health, till death do you part?"

Maria, with tears running down her face, managed to choke out, "I do."

"Then with the power vested in me by the state of Connecticut, I now pronounce you husband and wife. You may kiss the bride." As William and Maria shared their first kiss as husband and wife Julia and Mikey looked on, smiling. And while Julia was doing her best to be an optimist, she couldn't suppress a feeling, deep within her gut, that this union would somehow end up in ruins.

CHAPTER 38

William and Maria spent their wedding night in their rat-trap apartment in their slum-filled neighborhood in New Haven. After a passionate session of love making the two love birds spent the remainder of the night lying in bed, gazing into each other's eyes and discussing their dreams for the future. Beautiful children, great jobs, a big house and lots of money were all part of their future plans.

But these were just dreams, and deep down William and Maria knew that a lavish future would not be in the cards for them. Maria was fine with her reality, but William was taking it hard. It was his job to be the supporter, and to be a father who would have the answers when his future child asked the difficult questions. As dawn began to break, and Maria had finally fallen asleep, William lay awake, staring at the ceiling and mulling over the question he had asked himself a million times - *Why oh why do I have to be so stupid?*

As the weeks progressed after the wedding William and Maria settled back in to their daily routine. With Maria's waitressing job and William's part-time job taking care of Mikey the newlyweds were barely able to scrape by... barely. The bad news was William was unable to find another job to supplement his income. The good news was that this was the first job he had ever had which he not only enjoyed but felt competent doing. He loved taking care of Mikey, and on some level felt more like his friend than his babysitter. Furthermore, William liked being close to Julia. It was hard to pinpoint why, but William just needed to have the Pearlman's in his life. Not only was he independent, but now he was a married man with a child on the way. But Julia and Mikey just filled a void in his life that needed to be filled. Whatever the reason William just loved this family.

The situation was working out equally well for Julia. Although she had always been a hard worker (to say the least), she was putting in more hours now than ever before. Unfortunately there was no end in sight. The more she found out about the FDA approval process the more discouraged she became. *Why does the procedure have to be so difficult?* she asked herself daily. She had made it her life's quest to come up with a drug to help those with learning disabilities, and now that she had no one could benefit from her blood, sweat and tears.

At least the mayhem surrounding her project was finally beginning to quell down and, ironically, in a very small way, Julia actually missed it. There had to be a quicker way to get her drug to the market... but how?

CHAPTER 39

The expression, 'The honeymoon is over,' was certainly apropos in William and Maria's case. With Maria only two months pregnant, the realities of the couple's financial woes were hitting them hard. They were counting every dime just so they could pay their rent. The newlyweds were living paycheck to paycheck, and with a baby on the way that just wasn't going to cut it. After a day of working a double shift and running back and forth to the bathroom to throw up, Maria was not in the mood for William's excuses. While she knew he was doing his best she was not in the frame of mind to be reasonable.

"Will," she began, "I can't believe there aren't any jobs out there. You know we won't make our bills once the baby comes with you only working part time for Dr. Pearlman."

"Gee, that hadn't occurred to me. You really think we need more money?" William answered sarcastically.

"Don't take that tone with me, William Nathan Victory."

William knew Maria was mad when she used his full name. "You say you know, but I don't see you getting another job too quickly."

"You know I've been looking, what do you want me to do?"

"I want you to get a job, damn it! We need the money, and we need it now. How are we going to afford everything we need for the baby? I mean we'll need a crib, clothes, formula, not to mention the doctor bills. If you don't get another job we're in big trouble, Will."

Even though William knew this was all true, he didn't need any more pressure heaped upon his already sagging shoulders. "Well maybe I should go out and get one right now."

Maria began to realize that she was pushing William too hard. "OK Will, I get the point." But now William was the one who was going to be unreasonable.

"No, I don't think you do get the point, Maria," William said, his voice rising. "You know I'm looking for work every day, so why do you gotta ride me so hard?"

Maria quickly softened. "I know you're trying Will, and I'm sorry for giving you a hard time. It's just… I'm so nervous with the baby coming."

"I'm nervous too, babe," William said as he reached for Maria's hand. With this conciliatory gesture it was evident to both that this fight was over.

"You know I love you, Will."

"I love you too, Maria. And don't worry, I'm sure I'll find another job soon," William lied. And while William and Maria were both happy that their first fight as a married couple was over, they both knew that it wouldn't be their last.

CHAPTER 40

The following Saturday morning William arrived at Julia's house a few minutes before eight. After spending a few moments with Mikey, William entered Julia's office. William began the session by detailing the specifics of his recent fight with Maria. As Julia listened intently her brow furrowed. She knew that William and Maria's problems wouldn't go away until he was able to hold down a full time job and bring home his end of the proverbial bacon. However, she also knew that in his current condition he was unable to achieve this end. She was thrilled to have William helping out part time with Mikey, and she was paying him as much as she could, but she could only afford so much. With the realities of working primarily in academia and taking care of her brother she just didn't have any excess cash.

As Julia continued to listen to William's job woes her mind drifted to her drug. She just knew, way deep down in her soul, that the drug would be perfect for William. If she could just get FDA approval, William (along with the thousands of others that suffered from learning disabilities) could lead happy, productive lives. But FDA approval would take years if they even approved her drug at all, and Julia knew that time was one thing that William didn't have. No, William needed help now, and Julia's couldn't do a thing about it... or could she?

CHAPTER 41

As Julia continued to experiment with her drug she became more and more certain that she had made a breakthrough of monumental proportions. And to further bolster her spirits, the entire psychiatry faculty at Yale was behind her one hundred and ten percent. Even Angelo Campanella took a few moments out of his extremely busy schedule to call Julia every day and check on her progress. Julia couldn't help but be enthused by the normally reserved Angelo's constant praise.

"Julia, I know you're a far way off from pay dirt, but the progress you've made is extraordinary," he began. "I have hopes for this drug the likes of which this university has rarely seen."

"Thank you, Ang. And I want to thank you for all of the support you and the faculty have given me. It really means a lot."

"Not to be cynical Julia, but I'm pretty sure the reason everyone is so supportive is because they see a winner with this one. And as you know, everyone loves a winner," Angelo said through a smile.

"Well I'm appreciative nevertheless," Julia responded. "It's just that I never imagined the FDA approval process would be such a bear. Do you really think it will take years, Angelo?"

"Unfortunately I'd say that's a pretty fair bet. Not to worry you, but I've seen the FDA string projects along for years just to put the kibosh on them at the twenty-fourth hour. I know that's not what you want to hear, but I think I owe it to you to put it all on the table." Julia's heart sank as her end of the telephone remained silent.

"Are you there Julia?" Angelo inquired.

"Yeah I'm here Ang, but I'm not a happy camper," Julia said with a lump in her throat.

"Hang in there Julia. I'm confident that you'll reach your ultimate goal of getting your drug to the people who need it. It's just going to take some time."

But Julia knew that time was one thing that William didn't have.

CHAPTER 42

As the weeks progressed William still had yet to obtain employment other than helping out with Mikey. Maria was now twelve weeks pregnant, and thankfully as her first trimester was coming to an end the nausea was finally subsiding. The bad news was that without health insurance the Victory's had to pay their medical bills out of pocket. The result of this expense was that Maria had to pick up extra shifts wherever and whenever possible. As she worked harder and harder, and with her pregnancy progressing, she became increasingly fatigued. On the rare occasions where she wasn't working she was sleeping, and unfortunately it was putting a real strain on the newlywed's relationship. Maria and William were barely spending time together and all aspects of their relationship were suffering, including their sex life. It seemed like they never saw each other, but maybe it was better that way. When the couple did sneak a few moments together they spent most of it fighting, usually about finances. William knew that Maria was hormonal, tired and frustrated, but he still found it hard to sympathize. Why couldn't she understand that he was doing his best? He was so sick of people telling him to just try harder. Couldn't everyone understand that not only wasn't he smart, but he was just plain stupid? Why couldn't everyone just understand?

Over the next two months William and Maria's relationship continued to suffer. The couple that had been so in love just a short time ago was in tailspin. However, the one common thread that was keeping the relationship alive was the baby that would be arriving in a mere four or five months... give or take. And on this particular overcast Wednesday morning, William and Maria were fully united as they rode the bus to Mercy Memorial Hospital.

It was time for the big twenty-week ultrasound. Not only would they find out if the baby was healthy to this point but they would find out the sex as well, and the couple couldn't have been more excited. Did they want a boy or girl? They both agreed that it didn't really matter as long as the baby was healthy. As the couple sat in the waiting room that looked like it hadn't been updated since the 1970's they tried to be patient, but it was hard. They passed the time by discussing baby names. When Maria suggested William Jr. if it was a boy William became quite upset.

"No way!" William shot back. "I don't want this kid to be anything like me, not even his name."

"OK, OK," Maria reassured him while simultaneously trying to calm him down – there were many patients within earshot.

"It won't be William Jr., I promise."

Thankfully the tension was eased when the couple finally heard their name called. As William and Maria made their way into the small examination room the rather unfriendly nurse spoke.

"Take your clothes off and put on this gown. The ultrasound tech will be with you when she can," she stated as she closed the door behind her. Maria changed her clothes and the couple waited as patiently as they could, but the anticipation of the moment was painstaking. After what seemed like an eternity the ultrasound tech finally made her way into the room. Thankfully, she was a lot friendlier than the previous nurse.

"Hello Maria and William, I'm Dawn Adams, and I'll be performing your ultrasound today. Maria, if you would please lie back, we'll get started." She took out the lubricating gel. "This will be a little cold, but just relax and we'll take a look-see." Before William and Maria knew what hit them there it was… their baby was right there on the monitor for all to see.

"Oh my God," William said. Maria just sat there speechless, her eyes moist. Dawn, who had seen this reaction many times in the past, was nevertheless sensitive to the emotions of new parents.

"Pretty amazing isn't it?" Dawn stated with excitement.

"It's unreal," William replied.

"I have three of my own. I've been doing this for years and it never ceases to amaze me." As Dawn continued to move the scanner over Maria's belly the couple's eyes were glued to the screen.

"The first thing we're going to do is make sure everything is OK with the baby." As Dawn looked for all of the checkpoints of healthy development she detailed her every move to the parents, who were holding their breath. After about twenty nervous minutes Maria and William got the news they were looking for - everything with the baby was fine. But just as the tension appeared to be breaking Dawn turned up the heat.

"Do you want to know the sex of the baby?" Although William and Maria has previously agreed to find out the sex, now that the question was in front of them their minds began to race. William spoke first. "What do ya say Maria, do you want to know?"

"It's up to you, Will. I could go either way, so you make the decision."

"Let's go for it," William said nervously.

"OK," Maria said in Dawn's direction. "I guess we want to know."

"Are you sure?" Dawn asked one more time. William and Maria looked into each other's eyes, and they knew.

"Yeah, we're sure," they said together.

"Well congratulations you two, you're having…" Dawn paused for dramatic effect. "A boy!"

As William and Maria shared a kiss their heads were spinning. While Maria was wondering how in the world she was going to raise a boy, William only had one continuous thought running through his head - *Please don't let this boy be anything like his father.*

CHAPTER 43

As the euphoria of the twenty-week ultrasound wore off William began to feel the stress of his new role as a husband and soon-to-be father more than ever. He checked the newspapers everyday and went on a couple of interviews a week, but in the tight economy and with no high school diploma he wasn't having any luck. And to make things worse, he and Maria were fighting again.

On a snowy Saturday morning William sat in Julia's office and lamented his current state of affairs. "I just don't know what I'm gonna do, Dr. Pearlman. I feel so much pressure to get a job and be the supporter, but I know I just ain't capable of that. It's like this huge weight on my shoulders that just won't go away."

"I know things have been tough," Julia sympathized, "but you've got to hang in there. I'm sure things will get better," Julia lied as convincingly as possible. The doctor and patient continued to go in circles. And then, William ended the session by stating what Julia already knew.

"If things don't go better I think I'm gonna snap... I'm just gonna snap."

When Monday morning rolled around Julia was ready to take on her work week with reckless abandon. Unfortunately, things were not starting well. For one, her Saturday session with William had her worried. Truth be told she had been worried about him ever since she met him, but recently things appeared to be coming to a breaking point. Her training, years of experience and intuition told her that something had to give. And furthermore, things with the FDA were not going well. Not going well at all. She had already spent countless hours on paperwork only to get the recent news from an FDA bureaucrat that much of her work was 'insufficient.' Julia, who was never one to hide from a challenge, began to wonder if she would ever finish with the seemingly never ending paperwork. But after a few moments of self pity she jumped back into the battle and forged ahead. She would either get her drug approved or die trying - she just hoped she just didn't die of old age first.

CHAPTER 44

As the weeks progressed and winter turned to spring things, unfortunately, didn't change much. Julia was still mired in paperwork, William continued to work with Mikey for a couple of hours a day but still had no luck finding full time employment, and Maria was still working around the clock. The doctor had warned William and Maria that working too hard may put undue stress on the baby, but what choice did they have? Their bills were already pilling up, and with the baby due in just three months the struggling couple was desperate for the income. And then it happened.

As Maria was working the graveyard shift she started to get light–headed, and then she got a sharp pain in her uterus. The pain subsided and Maria chalked it up to Braxston Hicks contractions - a feeling similar to the contractions of childbirth but only feel the same, and have no real effect on the baby. But after several minutes the pain returned, and she began to panic. She told a co-worker, who dialed 911, and then she called William. Before she knew what was happening she was being whisked away in an ambulance to the hospital.

As the ambulance shot through the New Haven night Maria's contractions began to occur more frequently, and she could tell by the faces of the paramedics that things were not going well. A few minutes later the ambulance arrived at the emergency entrance of the Mercy Memorial Hospital and she was raced inside. The young paramedic barked more than spoke as he ran alongside the gurney. "We have a woman in labor here and the baby is coming!"

The baby is coming... Maria heard the words but could hardly believe it. It was like she was dreaming but she knew that she was awake, and this was definitely not a dream – it was a nightmare. Before she could comprehend what was happening she was in a labor and delivery room and a group of men and women in green scrub suits stood ominously around her. The doctor on call was unshaven and looked like he hadn't slept in days, but despite his appearance he was fully alert and in complete control.

"Maria, I'm Doctor Greenberg. How many weeks pregnant are you?"

"I'm only twenty-seven weeks. The baby can't be delivered now, can he?" Maria pleaded.

"I'm afraid so. You're fully effaced and ten centimeters dilated. This baby will be here in a matter of minutes," Doctor Greenberg proclaimed.

And just then, as if on cue, William came bursting into the delivery room. "Maria, are you OK? I got a call from the restaurant. What the hell is going on?!"

"Who are you?" Doctor Greenberg shot at William.

"He's my husband," Maria answered with tears in her eyes.

"Then you need to get into scrubs," Doctor Greenberg answered as he continued to examine Maria. As one of the nurses quickly escorted William out of the room Doctor Greenberg kept his focus on the patient. "Maria, if you feel like you need to push now would be a good time."

William came running back into the delivery room, his face white as a ghost, yet he dutifully took his place by Maria's side. William's head was spinning. Just an hour ago he was asleep in his bed, and now here he was about to have a premature baby. *How could this possibly be happening?* he wondered. But there was no time for questions, and Maria's scream brought him right back to the present. Before he knew what was hitting him he looked down to see the baby's head covered with mucus and blood.

"Just try and relax for a minute Maria. Don't push again just yet," Doctor Greenberg instructed her. He suctioned the baby's nose and mouth, then turned his attention back to Maria. "OK Maria, one more big push ought to do it."

Maria bared down with all of her strength and shrieked as she pushed one more time and there he was, a teeny tiny baby for all to see. He was so small and cute, but things were obviously not well. The little infant remained silent, and he appeared to be blue. Furthermore, the grave faces of the hospital staff answered any questions - this baby was in great danger.

CHAPTER 45

As baby Victory was hurried to the neo-natal intensive care unit Maria and William were filled with fear… and questions.

"Where are they taking him?" Maria cried.

"Will he be OK?" William asked in a panic.

"We won't know anything for a little while," Doctor Greenberg told them. "However, I can tell you that he's in very good hands, and as soon as we know something you'll be the first to hear it. But right now, Maria, we need to do a little more work. You still have to push out the placenta, and you tore a little during the delivery so I'll need to stitch you up." Maria was too upset, confused and frightened to put up a fight, and she dutifully complied as Doctor Greenberg finished up. William's head was still spinning, but he knew he had to be strong for Maria.

Eventually Maria and William were ready to go to the recovery room. As Maria was being pushed on a gurney down the long corridor toward her room she couldn't help but notice all of the new mothers and fathers blissfully happy with their new bundles of joy. Her heart broke as she listened to the healthy cries and gleeful laughter coming from the new families. When the nurse finally left (with a promise to give them news as soon as some was forthcoming), William and Maria were finally left alone with their thoughts and fears. The couple sat alone silently for several minutes with tears in their eyes before William finally broke the silence.

"He'll be OK, Maria," William stated unconvincingly. "He just has to be," he said, his voice trailing off. But with Maria too upset to speak the next hour went by in silence. Finally, after what seemed like an eternity, a man in a blue scrub suit with a solemn look on his face knocked quietly and entered the room.

"Hello…" he said as he peered around the door. "May I come in?" William and Maria, who were desperate for news, nearly jumped up to greet him.

"Yeah, come in, come in!" William nearly yelled.

"Mr. and Mrs. Victory, I'm Doctor Trietsch from the neo-natal unit…"

Maria couldn't contain herself and cut Doctor Trietsch off. "Is he alright? Please tell me he's OK," she cried.

"I wish I had some good news for you Mrs. Victory, but unfortunately it's too soon to tell. Your son was born three months premature and barely weighs two pounds. The next forty-eight hours will be crucial."

As Maria continued to cry William spoke up. "Can we see him?" he more pleaded than asked.

"Yes you may," Doctor Trietsch said as sympathetically as possible. "Unfortunately you won't be able to hold him, or even touch him for that matter. He's currently in an incubator for his protection." Doctor Trietsch turned his attention toward Maria. "Mrs. Victory, do you have the energy to see him now, or would you like to rest for a while first?"

Although Maria was exhausted from the childbirth, as well as a night without sleep, she answered without hesitation. "Let's go!"

The Victory's followed Dr. Trietsch through the maze-like hospital until they finally made their way to a room full of blinking, ticking and beeping machines interspersed with babies in incubators. As William and Maria made their way to their child the sight was nearly overwhelming. There lay baby Victory, clinging to life with all sorts of tubes and wires connected to his infinitely small body. He seemed to be gasping for air. While Maria looked upon her son and cried, William reminded himself that he needed to stay strong for his wife and son.

"Oh my God Will, look at him," Maria said. "I already love him so much! If he doesn't make it I don't think I'll be able to go on living."

"He's gonna make it, Maria," William said with all of the confidence he could muster.

"How do you know?" Maria said through her tears.

"I just know it."

And incredibly, William did know it. He knew that he didn't know much, but this he knew and believed with all of his heart. This baby was going to make it… he just had to!

CHAPTER 46

Julia came home from another long, tiring, frustrating day at work. Unfortunately, the scene at home was no better. As Julia made her way into her living room she found Mikey eating a box full of Twinkies with no sign of William anywhere.

"Mikey!" Julia exclaimed, "what's going on here? Where's William?"

"I don't know Julie," Mikey said through yellow, Twinkie-filled teeth. "He wasn't here when I come home." As upset as Julia was to see Mikey home alone she immediately panicked. It wasn't like William to simply not show up, and Julia just knew something wasn't right. Her gut told her so. She rushed to the phone and called William, and when there was no answer she called the hospital.

"Hello, Mercy Memorial Hospital," the receptionist stated cheerfully. "How may I direct your call?"

"I'm not sure," Julia responded with trepidation in her voice. "I was wondering if there was a patient there with the last name of

Victory?"

"One moment please and I'll check."

Julia waited, a lump in her throat and a pit in her stomach. As the receptionist came back on the line Julia already knew the answer.

"Yes, there is a Maria Victory in Labor and Delivery. Would you like me to connect you?"

But only silence remained on the other side of the line. "Hello… Hello, Miss are you there?" There was no answer as Julia grabbed Mikey and her keys and rushed out the door.

When Julia and Mikey arrived at Mercy Memorial they literally ran through the lobby to the stairs. There was no time to wait for the elevators. After sprinting up the four flights to Labor and Delivery the brother and sister were both winded, but they continued their quick pace until they made it to the nurse's station.

"May I help you?" the overworked nurse on duty casually asked without making eye contact.

"We're here to see the Victory's. I believe they were admitted recently."

When the nurse heard the anxiety in Julia's voice she quickly changed her tune. "Yes, they came in late last night. They're in room four-eighteen. It's down the hall on the right. But I should tell you that visiting hours are over in twenty minutes."

Maria lay in her bed half asleep when she heard the knock at the door. "Come in," she replied softly, expecting to see yet another nurse with the same news as always… no news. But when Maria saw Julia and Mikey she instantly broke into tears.

"Oh my God Maria, what happened?" Julia nearly whispered.

"I don't know what happened," Maria began. "I was working at the restaurant and I went into labor, and before I knew what was going on he was born. He only weighs two pounds. He's so tiny,

Dr. Pearlman. The doctors don't know if he's going to make it."
The gravity of the situation suddenly hit the women, and they both began to cry as Mikey looked on.

"I'm so sorry," Julia sympathized. "But with the medical technology that we have today he's got a good chance. You just have to stay optimistic - we all do."

"Where's William?" Mikey interjected. "I want to see William."

"He's in the chapel," Maria answered. "It's on the first floor. I'm sure he'd like to see both of you."

Julia and Mikey took the elevator down to the first floor and followed the signs to the chapel. The sparsely attended audience consisted of just three parishioners, with William sitting in the back row.

"Hi William!" Mikey blurted out a little bit too loud. For the first time in twenty-four hours a smile pierced William's lips.

"Hey there, Mikey. Hi Dr. Pearlman. Thanks for coming."

"How are you holding up, William?" Julia asked.

"I'm OK," William said bravely. "I know I ain't that religious or anything, but I thought it couldn't hurt… me being here, that is."

"It definitely can't hurt," Julia reassured him.

"Yeah William, God will help you. Isn't that right, Julie? God will help William, won't he?" Mikey asked.

"I'm sure he will, Mikey. If we pray hard enough hopefully God will answer our prayers." And for the rest of the night that's just what the three friends did. They prayed.

CHAPTER 47

After another anxiety-ridden day baby Victory was still fighting, and as the monumental forty-eight hour period came and went everyone breathed a huge sigh of relief. While the doctors cautioned William and Maria that their infant son was not out of the woods yet, they did concede that he had made it through the most tenuous moments, and that was doing as well as could be expected. After another day passed Maria was sent home from the hospital with the unfortunate knowledge that her baby would not be able to join her for several weeks.

However, now that things were looking up William and Maria agreed that they really needed to pick a name for their child. They had been putting off the decision for two reasons. For one, they didn't know if their son would make it, and two, they couldn't agree on a name. After going around in circles baby Victory still remained nameless.

After a long day at the hospital William and Maria were trying to relax at home when they heard a knock at the door. A strange occurrence, to say the least. Truth be told the Victory's hadn't had a visitor (with the exception of their landlord looking for the overdue rent) since they had moved in months earlier. As William went to the door he was simultaneously shocked and thrilled to see Julia standing in the doorway with flowers in her hand.

"Hi Dr. Pearlman. What are you doing here?"

"I'm here to check up on the two of you," Julia said with concern in her voice. "May I come in?"

"Sure you can. Thanks for coming."

As Julia made her way into the apartment even she was surprised at how shabby it was. Even though it was clean she couldn't help but feel like the place might collapse at any moment. She took a seat on a metal chair at the kitchen table and listened as William and Maria filled her in on the latest happenings. When the inevitable question of the baby's name came up, William and Maria embarrassingly admitted that they were unable to come to a decision. And then suddenly William had a thought, and he turned to Maria.

"Babe, what would you say if we have Dr. Pearlman name the baby?"

Before Maria could answer Julia interjected. "William, that's a very nice gesture, but I couldn't't."

But the idea made sense to Maria as well. "You've done so much for us, Dr. Pearlman. And we really can't come up with a name on our own. We'd really love it if you would name our baby," Maria said.

As William nodded his head in agreement Julia understood that the Victory's really wanted to bestow this honor on her, and she didn't have to think long to come up with a name.

"Well William and Maria, as you both know I'm Jewish, and a

custom in the Jewish religion is to name children after loved ones who have passed away." As William and Maria listened intently Julia continued. "One of the biggest regrets of my life is that I'm now too old and will most likely never have children of my own to name after my parents. Therefore, the name I would choose is Itzy. It's for my father who passed away several years ago. I realize it's old fashioned, but it would mean a lot to me."

William and Maria's eyes met across the table and they both instantly knew that this was the right thing to do. "Itzy Victory," William said.

"It's got a nice ring to it," Maria added.

"Itzy it is!" William announced.

As William and Maria smiled Julia had tears in her eyes. "Thank you so much," Julia said.

"No," William answered. "Thank you."

CHAPTER 48

Maria and William visited the hospital everyday for the next three weeks. Unfortunately the bills still needed to be paid, so Maria pulled double duty. She worked in the restaurant during the day and visited Itzy at night.

After an exhausting, interminable few weeks Itzy was finally ready to come home. The Victory's scraped up all of their pennies to buy a crib, diapers and some baby clothes, and because William and Maria lived in a one bedroom apartment Itzy would be sharing his sleeping quarters with his parents. Yet despite their financial hardships William and Maria were ecstatic. Although they were feeling the stress that all new parents know all too well, William and Maria couldn't believe they had a small yet healthy baby boy to love and cherish.

As Maria continued to work around the clock William picked up the role of Mr. Mom. Luckily for William, Julia was more than happy to have Itzy tag along during babysitting duty. Surprisingly to all, and mostly to William, he was a very good primary caregiver. Furthermore, he actually enjoyed it. He relished playing with Itzy, feeding him, and he didn't even mind changing diapers. As another week passed all was going as well as could be expected for the Victory's. And then it came.

Maria was going through the day's mail when she saw a benign -looking envelope with a return address from Mercy Memorial Hospital. She instinctively knew that this would not be good news and opened the envelope with trepidation, but what she found inside was worse than she could have ever imagined. She stared blankly at the invoice, hardly able to believe it - ten thousand dollars! With tears in her eyes and a quiver in her voice she called out to William, who came running.

"We just got a bill from the hospital for ten thousand dollars!" Maria exclaimed.

"But how is that possible?" a shocked William asked.

"I guess because Itzy was in the Intensive Care Unit for so long it just added up. But oh my God, Will, what are we gonna do? There's no way we'll ever be able to pay this! We can hardly pay our regular bills." As Maria began to cry William felt a pain in his stomach. The young couple continued to panic, and eventually went to bed not knowing what else to do. After several hours of staring at the ceiling Maria finally fell asleep, but William was wide awake.

After a sleepless night and then another, Saturday morning thankfully rolled around. William, who always looked forward to his sessions with Julia, was particularly looking forward to this week's meeting. William needed to unload the burden of his financial woes. He spent a few minutes with Mikey, then took his position on the couch in Julia's office. After some preliminary chit chat Julia could sense that something was bothering William.

"Is anything the matter?" Julia asked.

"Actually there is something on my mind."

"Go ahead, William. Let me know what's troubling you."

As William told Julia about his most recent monetary difficulties Julia listened intently. After bantering back and forth it was obvious to Julia that there was no conceivable way that William and Maria would be able to pay this debt. As their session came to an end no real progress had been made, but somehow William felt better.

"Thanks Dr. Pearlman. That was real helpful."

"You're welcome William, but we really didn't come to a resolution," Julia admitted.

"I know, but at least I got it off my chest," William stated. "For the first time in days I feel like my mind is kind of clear."

But Julia's mind was far from clear. She had a big decision to make, and unlike William, her mind was full of clutter.

CHAPTER 49

That night William and Maria were sitting at home with the television on, but neither of them were really watching. When a knock came at the door the Victory's both had a sense of déjà vu. Their premonitions were realized when once again it was Julia at the door. As Julia was welcomed into the Victory home she was all smiles.

"Dr. Pearlman?" William asked. "What are you doing here?"

"Is this a bad time?" Julia asked, now somewhat concerned.

"No, of course not," Maria chimed in. "You're always welcome here."

"I'm sorry Dr. Pearlman," William apologized. "I didn't mean it like that. I'm just surprised to see you, that's all."

"Well, I come bearing gifts," Julia said, her smile returning. "I was at home thinking when it occurred to me that I have yet to give you a present for Itzy's birth."

"Dr. Pearlman, you've done so much for me, the last thing you need to do is bring us a present," William explained.

"This is something I really want to do," Julia said as she handed Maria an envelope. William looked on as Maria opened up the card. When Maria turned pale William got concerned. "Babe, are you OK?"

"I'm not sure," Maria said, her voice shaking. "Will, look at this." As William took the envelope Julia continued to look on with that same smile on her face. When he opened up the card it simply stated, *Congratulations on a beautiful baby boy.* But when he looked more carefully at the check that was folded up within the card his expression turned to one of disbelief.

"Ten thousand dollars," he mouthed. He looked at Maria and then turned to Julia. "Dr. Pearlman," William stated, "this is super generous and all, but we just can't take this."

"Will's right," Maria chimed in. "It's an incredibly nice thing to do, but we just can't accept it. It's too much."

But Julia wouldn't hear of it as she shook her head. "This is something Mikey and I really want to do. We don't have a lot of close relatives, and we both think of the two of you like family. Please, we really want you to have this gift. It would mean a lot to Mikey and me if you would accept it and pay off Itzy's hospital bill."

As Maria began to cry William went to Julia and gave her a hug. "Dr. Pearlman," William began, "Maria and I don't know what we would have done if you hadn't come into our lives. Thank you so much."

"You're very welcome."

CHAPTER 50

As the weeks and months progressed Julia's work continued to forge ahead. Her hamster, Sigmund, was now perusing his way through mazes as well as or better than ninety-five percent of his contemporaries, and Julia was thrilled with his improvement. And while she was now as confident as ever that her drug could (and would) be able to help countless learning disabled individuals, she was extremely frustrated with her lack of success with the FDA process. After another painstaking day of forms and bureaucracy, Julia had had it. With nowhere else to turn she picked up the phone and dialed.

"Hello Angelo, it's Julia."

Dr. Campanella immediately sensed the distress in his friend's voice. "Hi Julia, let me guess... FDA hell?" he said with a laugh.

"How'd you know?" Julia responded, the tension now melting.

"I've witnessed it more times then I'd like to remember," Angelo said sympathetically. "Just try to remember Julia, it's not a sprint but a marathon."

"It's just such a pity, Ang. Here I stand, with a life's worth of work, and I finally make a breakthrough that could conceivably help millions and these idiots at the FDA are making my life miserable," Julia said, working herself up again.

"Unfortunately, Julia, there's no way around it. You'll just have to stick with it. But Julia, I'm always willing to listen if that helps any."

"A little. Thanks Ang."

"You're welcome Julia. Hang in there." And with that Julia went back to another frustrating session with a stack of papers and no end in sight.

Unfortunately Julia wasn't the only one who felt overwhelmed. Despite the temporary relief William felt when Julia bailed him out with Itzy's medical bill, things had not gotten any better on the job front. As the rejections piled up William's low self esteem continued to plummet. Except for the time he spent with Mikey and his one hour weekly session with Julia, all of William's time was spent taking care of Itzy. And due to the fact that Maria was working so much, William was a Mr. Mom for hours on end. Furthermore, to make matters worse Itzy had been crying a lot as of late. A trip to the doctor revealed that Itzy was considered a colicky baby. While that explained the crying, it didn't make things any easier for William.

There was some relief, however. He continued to get a lot out of his time with Julia, and Maria did take over when she wasn't working. However, Maria was usually too tired to be an effective mother and generally needed to sleep. William knew that he wasn't dealing well with all of the stress he was feeling. Every time Itzy would cry, which was often, William would do his best to sooth his son. Yet recently Itzy appeared to be inconsolable, and William was at his wit's end. And then, on a seemingly benign Tuesday morning with Maria pulling another double shift, Itzy began to cry for no apparent reason. Actually, it was more of a scream than a cry. William did his best to calm him down, but nothing worked. He wasn't hungry. He had a clean diaper. He didn't want to play. After about an hour and a half of an excruciatingly piercing crying baby William simply lost it.

"Shut up, God damn it!" he screamed. "Just shut the hell up!" Yet all William's yelling did was exacerbate the screaming. Before he knew what he was doing he turned quickly, clenched his fist and swung wildly. His hand shot right through the cheap sheetrock next to Itzy's crib. And just as William was about to cross a line of no return he looked into his son's eyes, and thankfully he came to his senses. He quickly left the room shaking. "What the hell is wrong with me?" he said aloud. He sat down on the floor in the corner of the kitchen and put his head in his hands, and this is where he sat for the next two hours until, mercifully, Itzy fell asleep.

Later that day William and Itzy were at Julia's house, where they were babysitting for Mikey. Thankfully Itzy's mood had improved, and he sat with his toys quietly as William looked after Mikey. But William was visibly shaken, and at eight o'clock that night when Julia got home she took one look at William and knew something was amiss.

"William, is everything alright?"

Normally William wouldn't be able to speak about something so disturbing without processing it through himself, but in this case he was so shaken by his actions that he shocked himself with his candor. "No Dr. Pearlman, everything ain't OK"

Julia glanced over at Mikey, who was now watching television. "Mikey," Julia said. "William and I need to spend a little time talking in my office. Will you be alright by yourself for a while?"

"Yeah Julie, I'm good," Mikey said without taking his eyes off the TV. As William and Julia made their way into the office William's mind was racing.

"William," Julia began, "please let me know what's going on." For a couple of moments William sat silently. He was too embarrassed (and even a little bit scared) to recap the day's events. But after Julia reassured him once again that he could tell her anything and she wouldn't judge him he began to spill his guts. He knew he had to, or else next time he might do something he would really regret.

As William recalled the day's events in graphic detail Julia kept her calm, professional demeanor, but inside her head it was a different story altogether. She knew that if things didn't change for William soon he might crack. After counseling William for about an hour she felt comfortable that William was stable… for now. But she also knew that unless something drastic happened things would soon spiral out of control for her counselee and friend. In actuality she was amazed that with all William had going against him he had kept it together this long.

No, something had to change, and it had to change in a hurry. As William walked out of Julia's office per usual he felt better. He thanked Julia, said goodbye to Mikey, picked up Itzy and quietly walked out the door. Julia plopped down on the sofa next to Mikey and stared at the television, but her mind was miles away. She knew she had a big decision to make - a decision that could change her life forever.

CHAPTER 51

After several days of deep, heart-wrenching soul searching, Julia sat across from William at their regularly scheduled Saturday meeting. William began, as usual, by recapping his recent trials and tribulations. After several minutes William could sense that Julia was seemingly in another world.

"Dr. Pearlman, is everything alright? You're, like, not here today."

"I'm sorry William. You're right, my mind was somewhere else."

"Is everything alright? Is there anything I can do?"

"Actually William, there may be something you can do. But you have to promise that this conversation will stay completely between you and me. You can't even discuss it with Maria. You see, it's not completely on the up and up."

William began to chuckle, but when he realized Julia was serious his facial expression immediately turned serious. "Really

Dr. Pearlman? You, not on the up and up? I find that hard to believe."

"It's true William. Let me explain." There were many times that, due to William's severe learning disability, he had difficulty paying attention. But this was not one of those times. As William remained transfixed on Julia's every word she continued. "William, as you know I've created a drug that has the potential capability of helping individuals with L.D. Individuals like yourself."

"I'd have to live on another planet not to know that. It was all over the TV. for months."

"But what you might not know is that it will most likely take years for the Food and Drug Administration to approve the drug for public use."

"What does that mean, Dr. Pearlman?" William asked, somewhat perplexed as to why Julia was telling him this.

"It means that most learning disabled individuals won't see the benefit of this drug for years... if ever."

"What do you mean, 'most'?" William asked. "Does that mean that some people will get it? Like some sort of experimental group?"

"In a sense, yes," Julia answered, her eyes now widening.

"I'd sure love to get my hands on some of them drugs," William offered.

"I'm happy to hear you say that," Julia responded. "That's what I wanted to talk to you about. I'm really worried about you, William. I'm worried about you and your family, and I think you know how much I care about you, Maria and Itzy."

"I sure do," William said as he started to realize where this conversation might be going.

"That's why I've decided to make you an offer." Julia paused for a moment as William leaned forward. "I would be willing to let you take this drug on an experimental basis under my very close supervision."

"That's awesome!" William nearly shouted. "I've been dreaming about something like this to happen my whole life. I can't believe I'm finally gonna be smart!" William was now standing up and pacing around the room.

"William, please come back here and sit down. There are a lot of risks, and I want to make sure you fully understand what you're getting yourself into."

As William sat back down Julia patiently and methodically went through all the possible risks involved. She made sure that William understood that this drug was highly experimental, and while she had had success with laboratory animals it had never been used on a human subject. There may even be side effects or other risks that Julia had never thought of. Furthermore, William would have to be constantly examined and be willing to undergo extreme scrutiny by Julia for his own wellbeing as well as for the sake of science. And finally, what she was doing was illegal and by many standards unethical as well, and consequently it would have to be highly secretive. But when Julia was done William would not be deterred.

"Dr. Pearlman, I hear what you're saying loud and clear, but this is something I definitely want to do. I know there are risks, but I've been dreaming about a chance like this my whole life. A chance not to be an idiot. I mean, if I could actually be smart…" Tears welled up in William's eyes. "Well I would do anything for that chance."

Julia knew all too well that this was something that could literally end her career. But she also knew that if something was not done immediately it could spell disaster for William and his family. Julia had weighed the pros and cons, and she knew that if William was willing to take the risk she owed it to him to give him the opportunity. With William looking at her expectantly, Julia finally spoke.

"OK William. I'm convinced that you know the risks involved."

"I understand completely, Dr. Pearlman."

"Then I think we can move forward. I have to prepare the drug for human consumption and then we can get started."

"Just tell me when and where," William said with a steady voice.

"I'll see you in my office at Yale first thing Monday morning. And remember William, not a word of this to anyone."

The doctor and patient shook hands, and William left the office with complete confidence that his life would never be the same. Oh how right he was.

CHAPTER 52

Julia spent the next two days manipulating her drug into a capsule form. By the time William showed up in her office early Monday morning Julia was exhausted but simultaneously excited and nervous about what was unfolding. With William now in her office she locked the door behind him and talked in a hushed tone. Before she could get a word in an eager William spoke up.

"What do I need to do, Dr. Pearlman? I'm ready to get started."

"Just wait one minute, William. I want you to take a few more moments to just consider what we're about to do. Have you really taken your time to contemplate what we're about to embark upon?"

"I have Dr. Pearlman. I understand that it's risky and all that, but this is something I really want to do." Julia heard a determination in William voice that she hadn't heard before, and she knew immediately and for sure how serious he was. She reached into her top drawer and pulled out a vile of pills.

"Are those them?" William asked.

"Yes, William. These are the infamous pills."

"How long until I'm a genius?" William asked with a light lilt in his voice.

"Actually the medication has to build up in your blood stream first, so it will take about six weeks to realize the full effects. However, after about a week you should be able to feel the drug working."

While William was slightly disappointed that he would have to wait six weeks to achieve his goals, he figured if he had waited twenty years what was a few more weeks. Julia pulled two capsules out of the vile and handed them to William with a glass of water. He took the pills in his hand and ceremoniously held them up in the air.

"Here goes nothing," he stated. He swallowed the pills, took a drink of water and smiled. "I feel smarter already," he joked.

But Julia was all business. "Remember William, you need to keep a diary of everything you're feeling. No matter how minute the detail, I want you to document it."

"I will Dr. Pearlman. I promise. Please don't worry, I'm positive this is all going to work out great."

"I wish I had your confidence, William," Julia said with a nervous smile. "Remember," she continued, "we'll meet every morning. You'll take the pills and we'll document your progress."

"No problem, Dr. Pearlman. No problem at all."

Julia hoped William was right, but as she forced herself to stay clinical all she could think about we're the multitude of potential problems that lay ahead.

CHAPTER 53

After only a couple of days of taking Julia's drug William could swear that he was already thinking more clearly. Julia chalked this up to a placebo effect, but nevertheless William was very optimistic. Furthermore, Maria was working so hard that she had no idea of William and Itzy's whereabouts. Consequently, William was having no difficulty seeing Julia every morning and keeping it a secret from his wife.

Just prior to starting their experiment Julia had given William a processing test. She surmised that because a processing difficulty was the result of the neurological disorder underlying learning disabilities, any increase in processing speed may mean that the drug was having its desired effect. On his first processing exam William scored extremely poorly, falling below the first percentile when compared to a national sample of participants his age. Julia decided it would be prudent to give William processing exams weekly to assess any potential progress. She had originally decided to start the exams after the second week because she assumed that the drug couldn't possibly have any worthwhile results after only seven days, yet after only one week William was so insistent that he was thinking more clearly that Julia decided to test him. To her surprise, William had made some real progress - he was now at the fifth percentile. It was far from where she hoped he would end up, but after only one week it was a promising result.

While Julia remained clinically reserved William couldn't help but get excited. "I'm telling you Dr. Pearlman, it's working. I tell ya, it's like my mind is more clear already." As Julia explained to William that this could be due to a multitude of reasons she couldn't help but get excited herself, and as the weeks progressed William continued to show more and more improvement.

After four weeks he was processing information at the fiftieth percentile and, incredibly, at the end of the six week period William was now processing information at the ninety-eighth percentile. Julia and William were nearly bursting at the seams.

"I feel incredible!" William exclaimed. "I've always wondered what it would be like to be able to think like a regular person. It's like I've got a whole new brain. Your drug works, Dr. Pearlman. It really works!"

Julia could hardly believe it. But when William suggested that she go public with the information Julia had mixed emotions. While she was thrilled with the results she knew that they needed to be scrutinized before anything could be written in stone. Furthermore, Julia wanted William to pass another test, this one of a real world nature. She wanted to see if he could hold down a job. And finally, Julia was hopeful that when her results were eventually revealed that the scientific public would be so excited that they would forgive her breech of protocol, i.e., foregoing FDA approval before testing on human subjects.

But Julia was a realist. For one, she knew that she could and probably would be in hot water with the FDA and medical ethics committee. And two, as a researcher she knew that she and William were far from pay dirt. Like with any new drug there were always potential unforeseen problems down the road. Julia just hoped and prayed that everything would work out. All she could do was hope and pray.

CHAPTER 54

On Monday morning, after her meeting with William, Julia found herself standing once again at the Human Resources office in front of Stuart Sherman.

"Well, well, well, look what the cat dragged in," Stuart said with a hearty laugh.

"Hi Stu," Julia said. "Long time no see. You look good Stuart. Have you lost weight?"

"Uh-oh," Stuart replied, "a compliment. What can I do for you, Julia? I take it you need a favor."

"Is it that obvious?"

"When you work in the human resources office you get hit up for a lot of favors."

"I'm sure you do, and guess what…"

"Yeah, yeah, I know," Stuart said with another hearty laugh. "Spill it."

"Well, I'm sure you're not going to be exactly thrilled with my request, but I was hoping you could give William Victory just one more chance."

"You're kidding right?"

"Believe it or not I'm serious. I know it didn't exactly work out the last couple of go arounds but I'm confident things will be different this time."

"How can you be so certain?" Stuart asked.

"Well, I can't exactly tell you, but I would consider it a huge favor."

"You know Julia, as I told you previously it's kind of a policy of the University not to hire people we've had to fire in the past. And need I remind you that your boy has been fired not once but twice."

"I realize this, but if there is any way you could bend the rules I promise you'll never get another solicitation from me again."

"Why do I get the feeling that I'm going to regret what I'm about to do?" Stuart said with a mock frown. As Julia looked on expectantly Stuart finally acquiesced. "OK, the University bookstore needs a cashier. It's not exactly rocket science, but from what I remember about William I'm not sure he'll be able to handle it. But for you, Julia, I'd be willing to give him one last try. But only because you're my favorite professor," Stuart said with a twinkle in his eye.

"Thank you so much Stu, I really appreciate it. And I truly believe you won't regret this."

"You and me both," Stuart said. "You and me both."

The next day William started work, and while he was nervous and apprehensive, somehow he just felt it would be different this time. As he walked around with the assistant manager he absorbed everything like a sponge, from the layout of the store to the return policy to working the cash register. It was like he had been doing it all for years. And at the end of his first day on the job he got the sincere praise that he had been waiting for his entire life.

"You're a quick learner aren't you?" It was an off-the-cuff comment by the assistant manager, but it meant the world to William.

After a successful week of work William and Julia were both beaming. The only problem was that now it was William who was pulling double duty. He would work at the University bookstore from seven to three and then run to pick up Itzy from daycare, which they started when he began working. Then the father and son would cruise over to Julia's to meet Mikey when he got home from work at the grocery store. Even though the ordeal had only been going on for a week it was already wearing William out. After discussing the situation with Julia she was very sympathetic.

"I realize it's been very difficult for you, William. I'm sure I can find a different sitter for Mikey."

"The thing is, Dr. Pearlman, I really like spending the time with Mikey, and I also feel like I'm helpin' you out. Is there any way Mikey could take the bus over to my house after work? I could make a copy of my key in case he beats me home, and if it ain't too much trouble you could pick him up on your way home from work."

"I could definitely do that, William. It would be helping me out as well. Mikey really likes spending the time with you, and I wouldn't have to find a new babysitter."

"Great," William said. "If it's alright we can start on Monday."

"Perfect. And William, I just want to let you know how proud I am of you."

"I couldn't have done it without you, Dr. Pearlman."

As the weeks progressed things were all roses. William was doing a terrific job at the bookstore, and the new arrangement with

Mikey was working out as well. The only sticky part was that while Maria was thrilled with William's success she couldn't understand how he was able to keep his job when he had lost so many others in the past.

"It's just different this time," William would repeatedly say.

"But how is it different?" Maria would ask.

"It just is. I'm sorry babe, but that's the only way I can explain it."

Although Maria wasn't completely satisfied with the answer she couldn't be happier with their new life. She was able to go back to one shift a day, and she actually had the time and energy to spend with her husband and baby. Things couldn't have been better.

CHAPTER 55

After several months Julia and William had settled into a routine. They would meet every morning (now at six due to William's work schedule) and continued to discuss everything. Julia had thought about publishing her results but the fear of the consequences she was sure to encounter kept her at bay. Meanwhile, another unexpected event took place. The assistant manager of the bookstore had to quit unexpectedly, and the manager offered William the position. William, Maria and Julia were all on cloud nine. The increase in pay was a definite bonus, but the real payoff was simply the fact that William's good work had been validated. For the first time in his life he was not only a competent employee, but he felt smart. He could hardly believe it himself. He felt smart!

William made another decision as well. It had always bothered him that he never received his high school diploma. After discussing his options with Julia he decided to take the test to get his GED. He studied for two weeks, took the exam, and aced it. After being named employee of the month for the third time he made another decision - he was going to start taking a couple of courses at the local community college. It was a decision Julia had helped William make, and furthermore she was willing to pick up the cost of the courses. Julia explained that how he did in an academic setting would enhance her research, and consequently she was happy to pay for it. William decided to take Algebra for his first course, primarily because he had always struggled with it so mightily in high school.

As William sat in his Algebra Two class he was eager with anticipation yet simultaneously apprehensive. Despite all of his recent success his old feelings of academic inadequacy came flooding back. But about five minutes into the professor's lecture all of his fears were washed away. He was soaking in every word, and it felt as if the lecture was designed specifically for him. It just all made sense. Furthermore, for the first time in his twenty years William actually volunteered to answer several questions. And he was right on the money each and every time.

At the end of the hour and fifteen minute class William was packing up his things when the professor sought him out. "Young man, you did quite well today. I have a feeling you just may be my star student this semester."

William was astonished. "Thank you," he managed to squeak out.

As William walked down the mahogany hall and out of the ivy-laced brick building he was elated. It was at this exact moment that he realized that this was as happy as he had ever been. In actuality, he never realized that he could feel this way. He wanted to scream from the rooftops... *I'm smart!*

CHAPTER 56

As the weeks progressed William continued to excel in all aspects of his life. He had mastered the assistant manager's position, his relationship with Maria had never been better, he was loving every minute with Itzy, and things were working out terrifically with Mikey and Julia. Yet despite all of his success, the one aspect of his life that was bringing him the most joy was his Algebra class at the community college. He had received an A on the midterm, and he was clearly the star student of the class. His relationship with Julia had even changed for the better. Julia was amazed at how insightful he had become. His metamorphosis was almost palpable. He was now able to speak to Julia on a whole new level, and Julia truly respected his perspective.

So when William suggested that Julia go public with the success of her drug she decided to give it some serious thought. Sure there might be some repercussions, William argued, but once the world saw what the drug could do there would be such a public outcry that the FDA would have no choice but to approve her work and, in essence, bring her drug to the masses. Julia decided to chronicle William's results for three more months, and if all continued to go well she would go public. She was almost giddy with anticipation.

Two weeks later, with the world as his personal oyster, William was walking home from another stimulating class of Algebra. The final was only a week away and William was fully confident that he would ace it. As William floated down the crime-ridden streets of his neighborhood he took a deep breath of cool New England air. And then it happened.

It was faint at first, and William thought he must have imagined it, but then it happened again. And it was louder this time. *You must kill.*

"Who said that?" William said, looking around. But no one was there. "What the hell is going on?" he mumbled. And then the voice came again, but this time it was magnified tenfold. *You must kill!*

As William covered his ears with his hands he broke into a cold sweat. He looked around one more time, but the road was clear. And then it hit him like a slap in the face. The voice wasn't coming from the outside world… it was coming from inside his head.

CHAPTER 57

William entered his home pale and shaken. Maria took one look at him and immediately knew something was wrong. "Will, are you OK?" a worried Maria asked.

But Will wasn't ready to divulge what had just transpired, and even if he was he wasn't sure he understood it himself. "I think I ate something that's got me sick," he lied. "I just need to sleep it off. I'm sure I'll be fine tomorrow."

As William slipped into the bedroom his head was spinning. After staring at the ceiling for hours he finally fell asleep. When he awoke the next morning he felt surprisingly refreshed, despite getting only a few hours of rest. He actually felt so good that he wondered if he had imagined the whole ordeal that had occurred just hours earlier. And when the next several days went by without incident William thought that he was out of the woods. *Maybe I did just imagine it,* he thought, more trying to convince himself than actually believing it. But then, seemingly out of nowhere, it happened again. He was on a fifteen minute break from the bookstore when then voice reappeared. *You must kill.*

Immediately William froze. He felt his body tense up, his heart raced, and the sweat begin to bead up on his forehead. For a split second a paranoid William thought that everyone around him could sense his panic. But as William caught his breath he realized that no one had a clue. After a moment of temporary relief William unfortunately came to the harsh realization that this voice in his head was not imagined, not a dream, but was definitely there. And as far as William could tell, it was not going away.

William did his best to make it through the day. He had to summon all of his newfound powers of concentration just to be an effective worker. Thankfully, mercifully, after what seemed like the longest day of work since he started it finally came to an end. Per usual, William met Mikey at the bus stop outside his apartment, and he did his best to give him the proper attention, but when Julia showed up at eight to pick up her brother William literally couldn't wait to get her attention.

Julia had barely gotten a foot in the door when William whispered through his teeth, "Dr. Pearlman, I really need to talk to you." She immediately sensed that William didn't want Maria or Mikey to hear him so she stepped back out onto the street as William followed her.

"What's the matter, William?" Julia asked.

William knew he could tell Julia anything so he just came right out with it. "I'm hearing voices in my head, Dr. Pearlman."

"What type of voices?" a very concerned Julia asked.

"You ain't gonna believe this, but they're telling me to kill." William could hardly believe what he was saying, but somehow he felt relieved to get it off his chest.

"William, we need to discuss this in detail. Can you come to my home office?"

"What will I tell Maria? I haven't told her any of this," William explained.

"What if I tell her that I need you to watch Mikey while I tend to a patient in crisis. Do you think she would believe that?" Julia asked, a sense of urgency in her voice.

"I guess it's worth a shot."

They went back inside and Julia explained to Maria about the fictional patient and the made-up crisis, and thankfully she took the bait. A few minutes later Julia, William and Mikey were cruising through the streets of New Haven as quickly as possible. When the threesome got back to Julia's large Victorian Mikey went to bed, and Julia and William made themselves comfortable in the office. It was going to be a long night.

CHAPTER 58

As Julia probed every possible psychotic scenario it became more and more apparent that her drug was most likely the culprit. William had no family history of psychosis. He was currently feeling no stress in his life. Truth be told he had never been more relaxed. Because of his alcoholic mother he never used alcohol or drugs. With every passing question the pit in Julia's stomach grew larger and larger.

After staying up half the night Julia unfortunately could come to only one logical conclusion: the voices that William was hearing were an unruly side effect from her drug. She felt physically sick. But when she explained her hypothesis to William she was shocked to see his reaction. While she had assumed that William would not take the news well, she was completely taken aback when he just lost it.

"So what the hell does that mean, Dr. Pearlman? You can't take these drugs away from me! I need 'em, I tell ya. Please Dr.

Pearlman, I'm beggin you. I can live with the voices. I'll just ignore them. Please, I can't go back to the way I was. I'll do anything," William said, now pacing around the room. Julia knew from her years of training that until William calmed down he would be in no position to listen to reason.

"William," Julia began, "I need you come sit back down and take a few deep breaths." As William acquiesced Julia continued. "Now, I realize that this is very upsetting news, but believe me when I tell you that a psychotic episode is nothing to take lightly. These voices you're hearing are very serious, and we have to try and put an end to them immediately." She inhaled deeply before continuing. "Unfortunately, the only logical conclusion I can come to is that these auditory hallucinations are a side effect of my drug. Consequently, the only prudent measure would be to take you off the drug as soon as possible." She paused to let the bad news set in, but William wasn't having it. Using his new ability to think clearly and efficiently, William came up with a counter proposal.

"What if I kept using the drug and you also prescribed me some of those anti-psychotic medications. Maybe that would do the trick," William pleaded.

Julia thought for a minute before answering. "That is one way we could proceed," she admitted. "However, William, I should tell you that it isn't exactly proper protocol. In situations like this the normal course of action is to cut out the maladaptive agent. In this case that would obviously be the drug."

"Please Dr. Pearlman," William said, pacing again. "Can't we just give it a shot? If it doesn't work then we'll take it from there."

Once again Julia was silent in thought. William did have a point, but it wasn't proper procedure. She couldn't help but fight her own disappointment, and she knew that if she didn't at least give William's idea a chance that a lifetime's worth of work may be going down the drain. She knew that William (and many others) were desperate for this drug, but she also knew that on some level she was giving in to her own selfish ambitions.

With William about to burst she finally spoke. "OK William, you've convinced me. We'll get you on an anti-psychotic combination of drugs right away, but you've got to make me a promise."

"Anything, Dr. Pearlman."

"You have to disclose everything to me. Even if you think it's insignificant I want to know about it. Do we have a deal?"

"Absolutely!" a relieved William nearly shouted. But he knew that, as much as he wanted to be faithful to his promise, he couldn't ever give up this life-altering drug. He wouldn't and couldn't go back to the way he was… no matter what.

CHAPTER 59

Julia and William continued to meet every morning at six, but now they had more to discuss than ever. Julia started William on a combination of several anti-psychotic medications that had proven effective in her past experiences. Yet she had to admit to herself that she was taking a shot in the dark. She didn't know how, or even if these anti-psychotic drugs would counter the effects of her drug. She was simply flying by the seat of her pants.

The next several days were uneventful. But then, out of nowhere, it happened again. William was at home with Mikey when the voice from inside his head struck again.

You must kill.

William's pulse skyrocketed and he once again broke into a cold sweat. Thankfully Mikey didn't have a clue, and William quickly excused himself to regroup in the bathroom. He splashed cold water on his face and breathed deeply. And as quickly as the voices had appeared they were gone.

Over the next several weeks the pattern remained the same - the voices would come and go, and William was resolved to do his best to ignore them. Furthermore, every morning he would tell Julia the same story - there were no voices. No problems. The anti-psychotic medications must be doing the trick because the voices were gone and they weren't coming back. While Julia was relieved something struck her as wrong. She wanted to believe William - she desperately wanted to believe him. But her intuition told her that something wasn't kosher.

Despite this fact Julia couldn't get herself to push William for more information. On some level her career aspirations were taking over, and she was struggling internally with ambition, ethics and friendship. But for now she was simply frozen, and for the time being was content to go through the motions. Unfortunately, Julia knew all too well that this was a recipe for disaster. She just hoped and prayed that it wouldn't blow up in her face.

CHAPTER 60

It seemed that the voice in William's head was appearing more and more frequently, but because he was doing his best to ignore it he couldn't be sure. Furthermore, William felt guilty about lying to Julia. But no matter what he knew that he couldn't give up this drug. Now that he had tasted paradise there was no going back.

But the voice and the lies were starting to take their toll. And it wasn't just the lies to Julia, but to Maria as well. Maria could sense that William wasn't himself. For one, she had never fully figured out how William had turned his life around. But not one to look a gift horse in the mouth, she decided not to push the situation. But now something was clearly wrong. He wasn't sleeping, he was aloof, and worst of all he was edgy. He had been in such a good mood for months, but now he was regressing. And to make things worse, whenever she tried to broach the subject with William all she got was a curt, 'Everything is fine.' She decided to just be as accommodating as possible in an effort to snap William out of his current funk.

William could sense Maria's uneasiness, but he was in such distress that he was having trouble just getting through the days. Thankfully, when he wasn't hearing the voices he was still able to concentrate and think clearly. But the fear of the voices coming back kept him in a constant state of turmoil.

And then, on a clear and calm late Tuesday night, with Maria working at the restaurant, Itzy started to cry out of nowhere (as babies are known to do). William picked up his infant son to console him. Suddenly, out of nowhere, the voice came back. But this time it was different. It was the same message of *You must kill,* but this time it was repetitive, over and over again. *You must kill! You must kill!* And now it was with an urgency. It was as if the voice was more compelling... more dire.

William held his son in a trance-like state. As the voice repeated itself over and over William began to squeeze. And as Itzy's crying became louder William squeezed harder. Then, as quickly as the voices had come, they vanished. Itzy's shrieking quickly brought William back to reality, and in a moment of déjà vu he put his son back in his crib and quickly left the room.

William was panicked. He never thought it could come to this. He was stricken with a fear that only a parent can know, and he instantly knew what he had to do. With Itzy crying in the background, he went to the phone and dialed Julia's number.

CHAPTER 61

Julia, per usual, was still up at the late hour, but she answered the phone with a hushed tone so as not to wake up her brother. "Hello," she whispered.

"Dr. Pearlman, it's William. I'm sorry to call so late but it's an emergency."

"Take a deep breath William, and tell me what's going on."

William felt that he had no choice but to be completely forthright with Julia, so he told her everything. He began by telling her that he had been hearing the voices all along, and finished with the most recent incident with Itzy. Julia couldn't say she was surprised, but she felt that pit in her stomach growing yet again.

"William, I need you to come over to my house right away so we can discuss this."

"I can't right now Dr. Pearlman. Maria is still at work and I'm in charge of Itzy."

"When will Maria get home?" Julia asked.

"In about an hour."

"OK," Julia said, taking control of the situation. "I'm going to stay on the phone with you until Maria gets home, and then I'll need the three of you to come over. I'll put together some sort of makeshift crib for Itzy and he can sleep here."

"But what will I tell Maria?" William worried.

"We'll have to tell her the truth at this point. I don't see any way around it."

William agreed, and the patient and doctor spent the next hour on the phone until Maria got home. Twenty minutes later the Victory's took a cab over to Julia's house. William simply told Maria that there was an emergency and that Julia would explain it. A perplexed Maria could see the fear in her husband's eyes, so she went along without any questions.

When William, Maria and Itzy arrived Julia had already prepared a sleep area for the baby. After putting him back to sleep the three friends went into Julia's office. As Julia told Maria the twisted tale of their experiment Maria's face remained expressionless. After Julia had told Maria all there was to tell the room fell silent. At first no one knew exactly what to say, but eventually Maria broke the silence.

"I can't say I'm totally surprised. I mean, I figured something was up because out of the blue Will was doing so much better. I obviously didn't know he was using the drug, but..." Maria's voice drifted off for a moment, and then she continued. "I just figured something was up."

"Well your intuition was right," Julia said. "And I'm sorry we had to lie to you."

"Yeah, I'm sorry too," William added as he kept his eyes glued to the floor.

"I should tell you, Maria, that I insisted that William keep this information a secret. If you're going to be mad at anyone please let it be at me," Julia offered.

"I'm not mad," Maria said graciously. "I know you were trying to help Willie. But what are we going to do now?" At this point Maria and William both looked to Julia, and she took over.

"Well the first thing I think we need to know, Maria, is if you can keep our secret. At least for the time being."

"You can trust me, Dr. Pearlman," Maria said with conviction.

Julia then turned her gaze to William. "I know you're not going to like this William, but we have to discontinue the use of the drug immediately."

"What?!" William nearly screamed.

"Will," Maria scolded, "the baby and Mikey are sleeping."

"It's just that I need it," William said, now slightly more under control. "Can't you just up the amount of the anti-psychotic medication?"

"Unfortunately, at this point I have to say no. These voices you're hearing are not going to go away, William. And this isn't something to be taken lightly. We have to nip this in the bud and cut our losses. And who knows, with more research, in several more years maybe there will be another breakthrough and my drug will be safe."

"Maybe!" William said, getting excited again. "In several years! I just can't wait that long for something that isn't even a sure thing."

"I'm very sorry, William. It's just too dangerous. I'm afraid the answer is no."

With nothing left to talk about William stood up and looked at Maria. "I need to be by myself for a while. Can you take care of Itzy?"

"Sure babe," Maria said compassionately. "But where are you

going to go? It's late."

"I just need to clear my head. I'll be home in a few hours."

As Maria looked at Julia for help, Julia turned her attention to William. "Are you sure you're alright?"

"I'll be OK," William lied, and with that he walked out the door to contemplate his return to the miserable existence that surely awaited him.

CHAPTER 62

Because Julia's drug had built up in William's system there was no immediate loss of cognitive ability. Unfortunately the auditory hallucinations continued as well. Consequently, Julia kept extremely close tabs on William for the next several weeks until the drug had completely worked its way out of his blood supply.

As the days passed William's psychotic episodes became less and less frequent. That was the good news. The bad news was that his mind was becoming increasing cluttered by the day. He began to forget things, make mistakes at work, and to make things even worse he was now more frustrated with his ineptitude than ever before. Now that he had experienced success, he couldn't tolerate failure.

About a month after ridding himself of Julia's drug things had regrettably regressed back to their original state. William had just been reprimanded by the manager of the bookstore for the third time in a week, and was walking home with his tail between his legs. *How could this have happened?* he wondered for about the hundredth time. He picked up the mail as he entered the apartment that now felt even more inadequate than usual. As he was sorting through the bills, there it was - an envelope with a return address from New Haven Community College. He tore open the perforated edge and stared at the computer printout. It read: William Victory – Algebra II: A+.

As William continued to stare at the grade it occurred to him that this was the first decent grade he could ever remember getting, going all the way back to grammar school. He was so proud of the grade he had just received yet simultaneously so disappointed in what could have been. Several moments passed as he sat at the kitchen table, and then the tears began to run down his face.

CHAPTER 63

It didn't take long for the inevitable to take place. After several more reprimands at work William got the ax. His boss couldn't understand how such a stellar employee had fallen apart so quickly. All William could say was that he was doing his best. Once again William found himself jobless except for taking care of Mikey. While Maria understood the reasoning behind William's downward spiral, it didn't make her feel any better when she had to start picking up double shifts again. And now William was more depressed and desperate than ever. He hated his life and couldn't stop perseverating on what could have been.

Now, with so much free time on his hands, William found himself daydreaming - a lot. He fantasized about what it would be like to be able to take the drug without any negative side effects - what it would be like to live the life he was so close to obtaining. But how? How could he get his ideal life back? It was a question he asked himself countless times every day, with no answer in sight.

Julia wasn't feeling much better than William. For one, she was extremely worried about him. She knew he wasn't coping well, and she wasn't going to take any chances. Even though their experiment was over she still insisted that they see each other several times a week. And two, she was immensely disappointed. Sure, there was always the chance that with some more work her drug could be altered to remove its psychotic side effects, but she knew that it was a long shot. For all intents and purposes a lifetime of work had seemingly gone down the drain. But to her credit, she was no quitter. She would take a week away from the drug and then forge ahead. To make matters worse she would have to figure out a way to pull her work out of the FDA approval process without causing suspicion. She reasoned that she couldn't ethically push the drug forward knowing that it could create such adverse side effects.

A couple of days later Julia met with Angelo Campanella. Julia had rehearsed what she was going to say many times, but sitting in his office, she was nervous about her ability to pull it off.

"Hi Angelo," she began, "thanks for meeting with me."

"I'm glad to, Julia. But I've got to admit that the voice message you left has me a bit uneasy. You mentioned there's some sort of problem with your drug. Please, fill me in."

"That's right, Ang. Unfortunately, I believe that the drug may lead to some undesirable side effects."

"Like what, Julia?"

"I'm not exactly sure, but my lab animals are acting unusual, and I think it's due to a side effect. I don't think I can go forward at this point with the knowledge that something might be wrong."

Julia studied Angelo's facial expression but was having trouble reading it, so she just held her breath and waited for him to respond.

"Well Julia, this is your baby. Are you sure you want to pull the plug on this project because of a hunch?"

"I think I am Angelo. For now, anyway. We'll see what the future will bring, and hopefully I'll be able to resubmit to the FDA in the near future."

"OK Julia. I'll support your decision, but please know that by taking this step, if and when you want to resubmit you'll be starting from square one."

"I'm aware of that, but I think ethically this is the only action I can take at this time." She nearly winced as she used the word 'ethically,' knowing that while she's had the best of intentions she has been far from fully ethical.

"I understand," Angelo said with sympathy in his voice. "I'll call our contact at the FDA and let him know of your decision. And Julia, I'm proud of you for putting your personal ambition aside for the good of the public."

Julia was so full of guilt that she could barely reply with a weak 'thank you' as she walked out of the office, carrying enough self-deprecation to choke a horse.

CHAPTER 64

Now that William wasn't working at the bookstore Julia asked him if he wouldn't mind taking care of Mikey at her house again. It would be easier if she didn't have to stop by William's apartment every day, she explained, and in actuality William was happy to get out of his dwelling. At least it gave him somewhere to go during the day.

As the monotony of daily life set in William's downward path continued. When he wasn't taking care of Itzy or Mikey he spent all of his time sleeping, and it didn't take a doctor to see that he was now clinically depressed. Julia decided to start him on an anti-depressant and to work with him during counseling. Furthermore, William found himself daydreaming more and more often, yet now the daydreams were taking on a new theme. Instead of simply imagining his life as it was several months earlier, William was now fantasizing about ways to get the life-altering drug back into his possession. He found himself thinking about ways to break in to

Julia's lab and steal the capsules. He knew the layout of the building. He knew where the guard's post was. He even knew the combination to Julia's office. In reality it really would be quite easy, he dreamed.

The problem was this daydream was becoming a constant topic of interest for William's sub-conscious. At first he just chalked it up to boredom, but now he was thinking about this plan so often that he began to get worried. He knew he couldn't act on this, but what if he did? He was no criminal, he rationalized. And furthermore, he would never take advantage of his relationship with Julia like that. But as this daydream perforated its way deeper and deeper into his psyche he knew he would have to come clean with Julia in session. At least if he got it off his chest it might help him stop thinking about it, he told himself.

That Saturday morning, at their regularly scheduled eight o'clock session, William knocked on the door and Mikey answered it.

"Hey William," an excited Mikey began. "Do you think when you and Julie are finished me and you can play?"

"I think that can be arranged," William said, smiling. Over the past several years William and Mikey's relationship had truly blossomed. Julia even confided in William that Mikey told her that William was like a brother to him. After chatting for another minute with Mikey, William went into Julia's office to begin.

"How are you today, William?" Julia said with the ever-present concern in her voice.

"I'm alright, Dr. Pearlman," William answered, trying to put on a brave face. "But actually there was somethin' I wanted to talk to you about, if it's OK"

"Sure William, go ahead."

As William revealed his constant daydream he described it in graphic detail. From the code used to break into the facility to disassembling the alarm to sneaking up on the guard. He continued to explain how he would tie up and gag the guard. He would sneak into Julia's office, steal the pills, then leave without getting caught.

As Julia listened to William's detailed explanation she actually found herself amazed that he could come up with such a well thought out plan in his current condition. However, she was also worried that he would actually think about following through on such a dangerous, and more importantly criminal, plan. Thankfully, after a long discussion, William explained that he would never follow through on his plan. It was simply a reoccurring daydream, he explained.

"I just wanted to get it off my chest," William said. "And you know what, Dr. Pearlman?"

"What's that?" Julia answered.

"I feel better already. Thanks for listening. I always feel better after talking to you."

"You're welcome, William. I'm fully confident that this is merely fantasy. I don't think you need to worry about acting on it. Frankly, I'm confident that you won't."

"I was hoping you'd feel that way," William said, relieved. "If it's OK Mikey and I are going to hang out for a little while, and then I'll be on my way."

"I'd appreciate that, William."

And with that Julia and William both felt better. *Finally,* Julia thought, *a successful session after so many disappointing talks. Maybe things will finally start to turn around for William.* And with that she went back to work, her heart feeling just a little bit lighter.

CHAPTER 65

Once William finished playing with Mikey he walked to the bus stop with a bit of a lilt in his step. It was amazing how simply talking to Julia and getting his thoughts out of his head and into the open could make him feel better.

While sitting on the bus William stared out the window and actually smiled. It was the first time he had felt like smiling in weeks. But when he walked into his apartment the smile was immediately blown off of his face. There was Maria, sitting at the kitchen table, crying.

"What's the matter babe?" a concerned William asked.

"Oh Will, I just got fired."

"How did that happen? You weren't even at work today."

"My boss just called me. Something about cut backs and increasing the bottom line, blah, blah, blah. Now what are we going to do? Neither of us are working. We have to pay the rent, buy diapers, put food on the table. Oh my God Will, we're in big trouble!" and with that Maria broke down again and began to sob.

"It'll be OK Maria," William said, trying to console her. "We'll get through this."

But Maria was in no mood to be comforted, and now her sadness and anxiety turned to anger. "Damn it Will, don't you get it? We're in big trouble, and you don't seem to give a damn. What's wrong with you?"

Now William was beginning to get defensive. "Nothing's wrong with me. I'm just trying to stay calm and figure this out."

"Is that because you're so good at figuring things out?" Maria shot back as sarcastically as she could.

She had struck a very exposed nerve, and she knew it right away, but it was too late to take it back. It was the first time in all of the years that the couple had known each other that Maria had insulted William's intelligence, and that was the one thing she knew that he just couldn't tolerate. Before she even had a chance to apologize the shit hit the fan.

"Well the hell with you, you bitch! Who the hell do you think you're talking to? If I'm not smart enough for you just say the word and we'll end this right now!" William screamed at the top of his lungs. He screamed so loud that Itzy woke up startled and began to cry.

"Will, you know I didn't mean it. I'm sorry," Maria said in a quiet voice in an attempt to calm her husband down. But William wasn't having it. He was beyond mad. She had never seen him like this, and it scared her. "William, you need to calm down. You're frightening Itzy."

But William was completely out of control. The stress of the last two months had been simmering, and now the volcano exploded. Suddenly, William shot for the door. Something had simply clicked in his brain, and he needed to get out of there.

"Where are you going?" Maria cried after him, but William couldn't even talk. He nearly ran out the door and slammed it behind him, not knowing where he would go or what he was capable of doing.

CHAPTER 66

The following morning Julia got an early wake up call. It was four o'clock when the phone rang, and she shot up from bed.

"Hello?" she answered hoarsely.

"Hello, is this Dr. Pearlman?" the strong voice responded.

"Yes, who is this?"

"Dr. Pearlman, I'm sorry to call you at such an early hour, but this is Detective Zalvan from the New Haven Police Department. There's been an incident at the University and your lab was involved. I'm afraid I need you to come down to the prescient immediately."

Julia's mind was swimming. "Who... what... a break in?"

"I'm afraid so Dr. Pearlman, and like I said the matter is pressing. Do you have transportation or do you need us to send a cruiser?"

Now slightly more alert, Julia's head was starting to clear. "I have transportation, but can't this wait until morning? You see I have a brother with Down's Syndrome who I care for and he's sleeping."

"Unfortunately, Dr. Pearlman, it can't wait. You see, there's been a murder."

"Oh my God," Julia said under her breath "Who was killed?" Her body tensed as she waited for the answer.

"It was the guard."

A shot of nausea shot through Julia's body as her thoughts immediately went to her previous day's conversation with William. "I'll be right down."

Julia woke up Mikey, who was not happy to be taken out of a deep sleep, and with a struggle got him in the car as quickly as she could. As Julia drove toward the police station her mind was spinning once again. *He couldn't have. There's no way, is there?* She grabbed her cell phone and adeptly steered with one hand while she dialed with the other. While it was now only four-twenty in the morning Maria's voice was alert.

"Hello, Will?" she answered hopefully.

"No Maria, it's Dr. Pearlman. I'm sorry to call you so early, but actually I'm looking for William. Is he out?" she asked fearfully.

"Yes, Dr. Pearlman. We had this huge fight and he stormed out hours ago. I've never seen him so mad, and I haven't heard from him since."

Julia's heart nearly stopped, but she composed herself for the time being so as to not worry Maria unduly before she was sure there was reason to do so. "I'm sure he's just blowing off steam and he'll be home soon."

"I hope you're right, Dr. Pearlman. But there's more," Maria added. "I went out looking for him, and when I came back I found a few red drops in the apartment. It seemed like it might have been blood."

"Blood?" Julia said. "Are you sure?"

"No I'm not sure, but I don't know what else it could be."

"Let's not jump to any conclusions. I'm sure he'll be home soon and we'll figure it all out then, OK?"

"Alright, but wait a minute," Maria continued. "You called me. Is everything alright?"

"It's fine Maria. It really isn't that important. I'm sorry to call you so early. Try and get some sleep, and please have William call me the minute he gets in."

"I will, Dr. Pearlman. Thanks."

By the time Julia hung up the phone with Maria she had arrived at the police department. As Julia and Mikey walked into the cold cement building Julia wasn't sure what to expect. She approached the front desk and told the clerk why she was there. She was quickly escorted to Detective Zalvan's desk, and she and Mikey sat across from him. Detective Zalvan drank black coffee out of a styrofoam cup as he addressed Julia.

"Dr. Pearlman, thank you for coming so quickly. As I stated on the phone there was a break in at your lab, and it appears that some drugs may have been stolen."

"What exactly happened?" Julia asked.

"Well it's an on-going investigation, so I can only divulge so much," Detective Zalvan explained. "However, I can tell you that there was a break in at the lab, there appeared to be a struggle, and the guard was tied up, gagged, and was asphyxiated. The perpetrator or perpetrators then apparently stole some drugs from your lab and left the building."

As Julia listened it was as if she had heard this story before. It was the exact scenario William had spelled out only twenty-four hours earlier. Then Detective Zalvan asked the question Julia was praying to avoid.

"Dr. Pearlman, do you have any idea who could have committed such a heinous act?" Julia was frozen in ambiguity. Since Detective Zalvan had called her about an hour earlier she had wrestled with whether or not she should reveal William as a potential subject. But when the question was in front of her it was as if she was caught completely off guard. After remaining silent for several moments Detective Zalvan spoke again, now sensing that Julia may know something.

"Dr. Pearlman, please understand that it's a felony to withhold information in a criminal investigation." Julia knew that she was already in too deep. Plus, she wasn't just putting herself at risk. There was always Mikey to worry about. If she got caught up in a legal debacle and actually spent a night or more in jail who would take care of Mikey? With the detective now staring her down Julia knew that she had to talk. But just as she was about to give up William it struck her.

"Unfortunately detective, I can't give you the information you're looking for due to doctor-patient confidentiality. However, I will contact my patient as soon as possible and try and convince this person to turn themselves in. I'm afraid that's the best I can do."

Now Detective Zalvan was annoyed. "Listen here, Dr. Pearlman, a man is dead," he said, raising his voice. "Don't tell me you're going to hide behind this doctor-patient privilege crap."

"I'm sorry detective, but I'm ethically bound to my patient," Julia said, now remaining calm. "Like I said, I'll do everything in my power to get my patient to turn themselves in, and I'll assist this investigation in any ethical way possible."

But Detective Zalvan wasn't having it. "Believe me Dr. Pearlman, you'll be hearing from us soon. I suggest you contact your lawyer."

"I'll do that. Good day, detective."

And with that Julia and Mikey stood up and exited the building.

Julia and Mikey got back home at about six o'clock and Mikey went right back to sleep, but that option was not a possibility for Julia. She was wound up, stressed and anxiety-ridden, and consequently spent the next several hours pacing around her living room. With her imagination getting the best of her, and not knowing what else to do, she finally decided to lie down on the sofa and close her eyes. And, incredibly, an exhausted Julia fell asleep.

Then there was a quiet knock at the door, and then another. With Julia and Mikey passed out there was no answer. The door opened and the visitor let himself in, walked to the sofa and stood over Julia. Feeling a presence Julia's eyes opened, and like hours earlier she sat up again with a fright. And there he was, haggard and looking like something that cat had just dragged in. There he was… William Victory.

CHAPTER 67

With Mikey still sleeping Julia quietly whisked William into her office. Before William could even sit down Julia attacked him with questions. "William, what have you done? Where have you been? How could you?"

"Dr. Pearlman," a perplexed William began, "what are you talking about?"

Julia could see right away that William really didn't know what she was talking about. She took a deep breath and tried again. "William, where have you been for the last twenty-four hours?"

"That's the thing," William answered. "I'm not sure."

"What do you mean you're not sure?" a frustrated Julia shot back.

"I mean I don't know where I've been. It's all kind of fuzzy."

"OK," Julia said, "why don't you start from where you do remember, and we'll go from there."

William sat still looking pensive for a few seconds, and then began. "Well yesterday me and Maria got into this huge fight. I was really pissed off. I mean, really pissed off. I started walking like aimlessly, not knowin' where I was going and just thinkin'."

"Thinking about what, William?"

"Just thinkin' about how miserable my life is and how it would probably never get any better. Thinkin' that Maria thought I was stupid and how I would never be able to keep a job. Thinkin' that I could never be a good father. And my mind was racing faster than it ever has."

"And then what happened?" Julia asked, now on the edge of her big black leather chair.

"Well I remember getting light-headed and seeing stars and then, all of the sudden, everything went black. The next thing I knew it was ten minutes ago and I found myself standing outside your door."

"And you really don't remember anything from the last day besides that?"

"No, I really don't. What the hell do you think happened to me?" William asked.

Julia once again sat quietly while she tried to make sense of this information. Her years of counseling, what she knew of William, and her gut instinct all told her that William was telling the truth, and consequently she could only come to one conclusion.

"William, I believe you have experienced what we call in clinical circles a 'dissociative state'."

"What's that?" William asked, now more confused than ever.

"A dissociative state is when an individual experiences a temporary amnesic period normally brought on by sudden intense stress. There are no long term effects, but the individual doesn't recall anything that happened to them during the entire episode, which could last from a few moments to a few weeks. What you experienced, William, appears to be a textbook case."

"Oh my God," William said. "That's pretty freaky. I wonder what I did for the last day?"

"Unfortunately William, I think I know," Julia said gravely. She spent the next hour detailing the events of the previous day. She began with the phone call she received from Detective Zalvan and ended with William's arrival at her apartment. When she finished she looked at William expectantly. At first it didn't seem to register, but after a few seconds his body language began to change and his brow furrowed. Then, suddenly, he turned white.

"Holy shit!" William exclaimed. "Do you think I could have done all of that?"

"I'm not sure, William. But I can't honestly say that I think you didn't do it."

"Holy shit!" William said again. "What do you think I should do?"

"I think there's only one thing to do now. I think we have to go to the police together and we both need to come clean, with everything."

"Everything?" William asked.

"Yes," Julia replied bravely. "Everything."

Minutes later William called Maria and she rushed over to Julia's house. After Julia once again recounted the torrid tale of the previous twenty-four hours, to Maria this time, she woke up Mikey for the second time that day and it was back to the police station… to confess.

CHAPTER 68

Detective Zalvan was surprised to see Julia back at his desk so quickly, but he was even more surprised as she recounted the events of the past several years. Julia started with meeting William at John F. Kennedy high school. She went on to describe every detail of the experiment with her drug, and finished with her hypothesis that William had just experienced a dissociative state and therefore, if he had committed the crime at the lab (and that was a big 'if'), he shouldn't, according to Julia, be held criminally responsible.

Julia actually felt relieved to be getting all of this off of her chest, but Detective Zalvan was incredulous. He could hardly believe the tale he had just been told. After composing his thoughts he spoke firmly and with authority.

"Dr. Pearlman, I believe you have some explaining to do, but I don't think that it falls under my jurisdiction. As for you Mr. Victory, you're under arrest pending an investigation." As Detective Zalvan read William his rights Maria began to weep, but

Julia remained in control.

"Don't worry William," she said calmly. "I'll get my lawyer down here as soon as possible. Just hang in there."

As William was being put into handcuffs he addressed Maria. "Don't worry babe, I'll be OK"

"We'll all be fine," Julia said, putting her hands on Maria's shoulders. "Just take care of yourself, and I'll get you out of here as soon as humanly possible."

As Detective Zalvan took William to the booking area in the back of the police department Julia, Maria and Mikey exited the building in a state of utter disbelief. *How had it all gone so wrong so fast?*

With William behind bars the threesome made their way back to Maria's apartment, primarily because it was closer to the police department. Julia immediately called her lawyer and explained the situation. As Attorney Brian Herman listened to her account of the pertinent facts Julia could almost hear his jaw drop. When she finally finished Attorney Herman could hardly believe what he had just heard, but kept his professional demeanor.

"Julia, the first thing we need to do is get a judge to set bail. I'm going to get down to the police station right now and meet William. As soon as I'm able to I'll give you a call with an update. For now, all I can recommend doing is remaining calm, and try not to worry too much."

"OK Brian, I appreciate it."

Julia hung up the phone, recounted the conversation to Maria, then suggested that she try and get some sleep. As Maria went to her bedroom to lie down Julia went back to the phone. She would now make the phone call that she knew was inevitable but had nevertheless been dreading for the last year.

CHAPTER 69

Julia listened to the ring on the other end of the phone with a lump in her throat and that ever-present pit in her stomach. And when the answer came, "Hello, Angelo Campanella," she actually felt a little bit nauseas.

"Hi Angelo, it's Julia. Do you have a few minutes?"

"Sure Julia, what can I do for you?"

"I actually wanted to talk to you about my research. I'm afraid I haven't been completely upfront with you."

"What do you mean, 'not upfront?'" Angelo asked with curiosity in his voice.

"Well the reason I pulled my drug from FDA approval was because I actually had proof that the drug caused some serious side effects. It wasn't just a hunch like I indicated."

"I'm listening…" Angelo said with concern.

"To be totally honest, I administered the drug to a human subject."

"What are you talking about, Julia? Is this some kind of joke?"

"I'm afraid not, Angelo. One of my clients has a severe learning disability and was desperate. After explaining all of the risks, which I should add, he completely understood, he began taking the drug. And it had marvelous effects at first. Unfortunately, this subject eventually began having auditory hallucinations, and that's how I knew that there were side effects."

She waited for Angelo's reaction, but none was forthcoming. For a brief moment she thought that perhaps Angelo wouldn't be that upset. But then it came.

"What the hell could you have possibly been thinking?!" Angelo nearly screamed. "What you did was not only unbelievably unethical, but it was extremely dangerous as well. I thought I knew you, Julia, after all of these years, but now I don't know what to think. I just can't believe you could do something so irresponsible. Please tell me what you were thinking."

"I don't know Angelo. I wish I could say that I was thinking solely about my patient, but truth be told I guess I have to admit that personal ambition played a role. I feel terribly about what I've done, and if I could take it back I would, but unfortunately that's not possible. I'm truly sorry," Julia said with complete sincerity. But Angelo was in no mood for compassion.

"And don't even tell me that this patient of yours was the one who committed the break in and murder at the lab?"

"I wasn't aware that you knew about that yet, but there is a chance that he is the one responsible. He's currently being questioned down at the New Haven Police Station."

"I just can't believe this, Julia. I'm sure you know that there will be severe repercussions."

"What kind of repercussions?" Julia asked.

"To be honest I'm really not sure yet. I'll have to let the

University president know what's going on. The ethics board will surely get involved. And unfortunately there may be a suspension or even revocation of your license to practice medicine. But that's something for the state medical board to consider." As Angelo was spelling out the potential reprimands even he couldn't help but now feel badly for Julia, and he softened just a little. "Also Julia, don't be surprised if the newspapers and television networks get involved. They're sure to get wind of this, as it is a somewhat sensational story."

Julia just listened in silence. While she knew she was in for an unpleasant ride, hearing Angelo present such a scenario really made it all hit home. Now it was real and Julia couldn't help but begin to cry. Angelo listened to his friend break down on the other end of the phone, and was now fully compassionate.

"Listen Julia, I know things aren't looking very good right now, and despite that fact that I don't agree with what you've done you are my friend and you've got an impeccable track record up 'til now. I promise I'll do my best to intervene on your behalf and help you through this tough time."

As Julia began to compose herself all she could do was whimper back a soft, "thank you Angelo." And with that there was nothing left to say. But with the click of the phone came a knock on the door. Julia quickly threw some cold water on her face and went to answer the door, only to find a fleet of police officers and detectives waving a search warrant in her face.

CHAPTER 70

Julia immediately went to wake Maria, who was already up due to all of the commotion. There were twelve members of the police force in all, and they were diligently looking through every nook and cranny of the small apartment. After about twenty minutes of mayhem one of the officers found something of interest.

"Detective," he called out. "It's me, Johnson. I think I just found the missing drugs."

Detective Perry was a tall, thin man with a mop of curly hair, and he was the lead detective at the apartment. He quickly made his way to the bathroom, followed by Julia and Maria. Detective Perry examined the vile of drugs and presented them to Julia.

"Dr. Pearlman, are these the missing drugs in question?"

Julia knew that the last thing she could do with all of the trouble she was already in was to lie. "They are," she answered as she looked at Maria, who appeared devastated.

"Hey detective," Johnson said again, "take a look at this."

Johnson was pointing to a small red stain behind the sink on the broken porcelain tile. "It looks like blood to me," Johnson pointed out proudly and authoritatively. Maria had previously cleaned up most of the blood but had apparently missed a spot or two. Furthermore, it never occurred to her to check the medicine cabinet for the drugs.

"Take a sample of that and get it to the lab right away," Detective Perry ordered. Although the investigation apparently now had enough evidence in hand they spent the next several hours tearing through the rest of the apartment, but they found nothing further of relevance. After the police finally left Julia instructed a physically and emotionally spent Maria to rest while she and Mikey made their way back to the police station to check on Attorney Herman and William.

Unfortunately, Attorney Herman didn't have any good news for Julia. "First of all," the attorney began, "William will have to spend the night in jail. We can't get a bond hearing until the morning. Secondly, he's not giving me much to go on. I know you told me that William most likely experienced a dissociative state, and I believe I fully understood your explanation. However, I've got to tell you Julia that if the state ends up prosecuting William with murder, and right now I'd say there's a good chance they will, a dissociative state defense, or in other words a not guilty plea by reason of temporary insanity, will have a tough time holding up in court. And lastly, I've got to warn you that this may be a long, drawn out case which could cost you tens of thousands of dollars in legal fees. I just want to let you know that because William could always ascertain the services of the public defender at no charge."

"I understand that Brian but William needs the best right now, and I'm willing to pay whatever I need to see that he gets it."

"I can appreciate that Julia, and my firm and I will do

everything in our power to see that William gets the best legal representation possible."

"Thank you, Brian. I know that you will," Julia acknowledged. "So what do we do now?"

"I'm going to go back to my office and prepare for tomorrow's bond hearing. If you'd like you can go spend a few minutes with William, and then I suggest that you and Mikey go home and get some rest. You look exhausted."

A few minutes later Julia and Mikey were escorted to the visiting area where they sat across from William, divided by a glass partition. Julia sat down and took the phone while Mikey stood behind her. William then picked up the phone on his end and spoke. "Hi Dr. Pearlman. Thanks for coming and getting me that lawyer," he said somberly.

"You're welcome William. How are you holding up?" Julia asked, already knowing the answer.

"I've been better. How's Maria doin'?"

"She's doing as well as can be expected," Julia said. "However William, I should tell you that the police were just at your apartment with a search warrant, and they found a few things."

"Like what?" William said, oblivious to what Julia had in store for him.

"They found the missing drugs from the lab and a red spot on the floor that looked like blood," Julia said, almost apologetically.

"Oh my God!" William exclaimed. "I can't believe it. I must have done it. I must have stolen the drugs and killed the guard," he said, a little bit too loudly.

"Shhh," Julia warned. "Someone's going to hear you."

"I don't care. I never thought I could do something like this."

"Take a deep breath, William. We don't even know for sure that you're the one who committed this crime."

"Come on, Dr. Pearlman. It don't exactly look very good."

"Maybe not, William, but let's say for arguments sake that you did commit this crime. It wouldn't have been your fault. You weren't in a conscious state of mind, and it doesn't take a lawyer to understand that you're not legally guilty under a condition such as this."

"Tell that to the guard's family," William said, his free hand covering his face. "I just can't believe that I'm a murderer."

And with that realization there was nothing left to say. William motioned to the officer on duty that he was ready to go back to his cell and left utterly defeated, without so much as a goodbye.

CHAPTER 71

The next morning Julia awoke early after a restless night. She was in no mood to get out of bed but forced herself to do so, knowing that it would be mentally unhealthy to simply lie there and worry. She dragged herself to the front door to get the paper and there it was, plastered across the front page: 'Doctor Uses Patient as Guinea Pig.'

Julia gasped as she stared at the headline. She looked up and down the street, not knowing exactly what to expect, and quickly scurried back inside and shut the door behind her. She devoured the article, which came complete with her faculty picture. Although there were a few minor mistakes she was amazed at how accurate and informative the article was. From her experiment, to the theft and murder, to having William in custody the article basically told the whole story. She was devastated but not surprised. After confessing to Detective Zalvan she knew the information would be part of the public record, but seeing it in print made her sick to her stomach nonetheless.

It didn't take long for the phone to start ringing off the hook. Several calls were from family and friends who couldn't believe the story was true, but most of the calls came from reporters looking for follow up information. After several 'no comments' Julia finally decided that the only thing she could do was to call the university and tell them she wasn't coming in for the next few days and to leave the phone off the hook. For the time being Julia would hide out at home and only leave the house to visit Maria and William.

Later that day Julia left to go to William's bail hearing and, unlike earlier that morning, the road was no longer clear. Julia literally had to push her way through the mass of reporters that had staked themselves outside of her house. After several more 'no comments' she got into her car and drove to the courthouse. Unfortunately for Julia when she got there it was more of the same, with reporters and television crews everywhere. Julia wore her sunglasses, sleeked her way into the courtroom and thankfully found a seat in the back of the room without arising suspicion.

A few minutes later William came into the courtroom wearing an orange jumpsuit, and everyone rose to greet the Honorable Gorham Scott Fisher. Judge Fisher was an ornery fellow who had been behind the bench for too many years and had no patience left for the tedious judicial process.

"Be seated," he said abruptly. "Bailiff, let's get started. What's the first case on the docket?"

The Bailiff read from the ledger, although everyone already knew what was coming. "The state of Connecticut vs. William Victory."

"Counselor," Judge Fisher stated ominously, "state your case."

The District Attorney, Marc Stoler, normally didn't make his way to a simple bail hearing, but with the media out in full force he wasn't one to turn down the spot light. There were rumors that the District Attorney would be running for Governor one day.

Attorney Stoler stood up importantly and cleared his throat. "Your honor, William Victory has been accused of breaking into a lab at Yale University, stealing some very sensitive drugs, and killing a guard in the process!" he said emphatically, pointing his finger up in the air for effect. "The crime lab informed me that the missing drugs were found in the defendant's medicine cabinet and a drop of blood, which has just recently been confirmed to be from the deceased guard, was also found in the bathroom of the accused. Your honor," Attorney Stoler said louder than need be, "this is a dangerous man. Consequently, the state is requesting that the defendant be held without the chance for bail."

With the mass of reporters taking down every word, Judge Fisher turned his attention toward Attorney Herman. "Counselor, state your case," he said with what sounded like a bit of disdain in his voice.

Brian Herman had been involved in hundreds of bail hearings in his career, but none with the notoriety involved here, and he was admittedly a little bit nervous. "Your honor," he began, "my client has no criminal record. He has been a member of the community for his whole life, and furthermore, his wife and child live here. He is far from a flight risk, and we therefore respectfully request that bail be waived."

As the courtroom teamed with excitement Judge Fisher spoke quickly and with authority.

"Due to the gravity of the crime in question bail is set at one million dollars."

And with the smack of his gavel William's fate for the next several months was sealed. With a bail set that high William Victory would remain behind bars.

CHAPTER 72

The 'Victory Case', as it came to be known, had gained national attention. Media from all over the country had camped out outside of Julia's house and Maria's apartment. They were relentless. Even Mikey couldn't avoid their barrage of questions. Julia and Maria couldn't even leave their places of residence except to visit William, and because Maria didn't have a job she was eventually evicted. With nowhere else to go Julia took Maria and Itzy in. Julia took a leave of absence from the University. She rationalized that with the media harassing her she would never be able to get any work done anyway, and she needed the time to devote herself fully to William. Furthermore, due to the disruption the media was causing to the New Haven legal system the case was given priority status, and was consequently fast tracked.

To make matters worse William was not doing well behind bars. Because his case had gained so much attention he was kept away from the other prisoners for his own protection.

Unfortunately, the isolation only served to add to his depressed state. With the weight of the world now on his shoulders his mind was more cluttered than ever before. He actually even had a difficult time concentrating during routine conversations. On Julia's daily visits she did her best to help him through his psychological stress, but with her allotted visits relegated to a half an hour and having to converse through a glass partition it was difficult to make progress.

Attorney Herman was putting in a lot of time and consequently billing a lot of hours. A month into the proceedings Julia's legal bill was already thirty thousand dollars. With no income coming in, and with the added expense of having to take care of Maria and Itzy as well as her brother, Julia was eating up a lifetime's worth of savings rather quickly. And just when Julia thought she had hit rock bottom she received another blow. When Angelo Campanella made his way through the media blitz to visit Julia at home she knew it couldn't be a good sign.

"Hi Julia," Angelo began. "I'm sorry to stop by unannounced. Do you have a few minutes?"

"Sure, I guess," Julia said with trepidation in her voice.

"I'm afraid I have some bad news." Angelo paused before continuing as Julia braced for the worst. "The University ethics committee has determined that your actions with Mr. Victory are cause for dismissal from the University faculty."

Julia was shocked. Although she had expected some sort of disciplinary action she never thought it would come to an out and out firing.

"But Angelo, I have tenure. I've been a professor in good standing for over fifteen years. Isn't there any way…" But Angelo cut her off.

"I'm so sorry, Julia. I did everything I could, but the

committee's decision is final. I'm sorry."

Julia immediately knew that it was useless to persist. "I understand, Angelo. I appreciate your efforts on my behalf."

And with that the two long time colleagues and friends both knew that there was nothing left to say. As Angelo exited out the front door to the photographer's flashing lights Julia broke down into tears.

"What am I going to do now?" she said aloud. Her life was in a tailspin, and it was only going to get worse.

CHAPTER 73

Because William's case was to move along quickly there wasn't a lot of time to absorb all of the information Attorney Herman was trying to hammer into his head. While Mr. Herman was a patient man he didn't truly understand what a learning disability entailed, and consequently he became frustrated when William just didn't seem to get it.

"William, I really need you to pay attention. This is very important information, and I'm getting the feeling that you're not fully understating the gravity of this situation," Brian had said more than once.

William, who never felt comfortable feeling stupid, just nodded his head and did his best, but with the pre-trial motions only a couple of days away he was more confused than ever. His head was spinning, and he just knew he was going to screw things up, just like always. William, who was not a religious person by nature, found himself praying to God every night for guidance. He needed a miracle.

After a weekend in jail William woke up from another restless night, dreading his first face-to-face interactive meeting with the District Attorney. Attorney Herman had prepped William as well as he could, but he sensed that William was unprepared and it worried him. These pre-trial examinations would have a large bearing on the trial and William was scared stiff, which didn't help his ability to concentrate and process the questions that were sure to be fired at him.

As William sat in a conference room at the prison with Attorney Herman they discussed some last minute information. "Now remember William, just answer the District Attorney's questions as specifically as possible. Try to get right to the point, and don't give him anything more than he asks for. Do you understand?" Brian asked.

"I think so," William said without much confidence. Just then the stenographer and Attorney Stoler entered the room, an air of importance surrounding him.

"Good day, Attorney Herman," the District Attorney said without looking at William. "Are we ready to get started?"

"We are," Brian answered. William was petrified, and the District Attorney could smell blood. As he started with the defendant he asked some rudimentary questions such as William's name, age and home address. But when it was obvious that William was having some difficulty answering even these questions Attorney Stoler had to suppress a smile. This was going to be easier than he thought.

After a few more prerequisite questions it was time to go in for the kill. As William stumbled over and over again the District Attorney nearly growled as Brian tried in vain to stop the bleeding. After nearly three hours of agony the debacle was over. William had done everything Attorney Herman had asked him not to do - he had elaborated on answers, contradicted himself, and worst of all he just about admitted his guilt. When Attorney Stoler finally walked out of the room Brian could only shake his head, and William felt like crying. They were behind the eight ball already and the trial was only weeks away.

CHAPTER 74

The Victory case, with all of its twists and turns, now had the public vying for more, and consequently the media was in a feeding frenzy. There were daily articles and news reports, and everyone who was even remotely involved with the participants were being heavily solicited for interviews. And as hard as this was on William, for Julia and Maria the worst part came from the tabloid press. It was bad enough that the 'reputable' papers got half of the facts wrong, but the tabloids seemed to just make up the stories as they went along. And while William and Maria took the stories hard, they really hit Julia where she lived. After spending a whole career trying to build up her reputation it was being ripped to shreds in a matter of moments, and there was nothing she could do but watch it happen.

As the trial got closer and closer the circus-like atmosphere was out of control. Julia and Maria bunkered down in Julia's Victorian home as they found it difficult to leave the house without getting completely overwhelmed. However, they made sure to continue to visit William daily, and Julia was on the phone with Attorney Herman several times a day as well. With no money coming in and the legal bills continuing to skyrocket Julia had no other choice. She thought long and hard, but with no other alternative she took out a second mortgage on her house.

With the pressure mounting Julia received a piece of certified mail. *Now what?* she said to herself. As she carefully opened it she pulled out the formal letter and read it slowly:

Dear Dr. Julia Pearlman,

The State of Connecticut Medical Ethic's committee hereby requests your presence on Tuesday, July 29th at the Hartford, Connecticut Town Hall Room 202 at precisely 9:00AM. The committee will then determine if a reprimand is necessitated, and if so to what extent the aforementioned reprimand will affect your medical licensure status.

Sincerely,
Kevin Fitzgerald, M.D.
Ethics Committee President

Julia reread the letter three times. Her mind raced with thoughts of the worst, but she steadied herself and decided to be positive. She would present her best case and let the chips fall where they may. Things were already so out of control that this was just one more log to throw on top of the fire. After having to sit by idly and watch the legal proceedings take their course Julia actually felt good that she could finally do something proactive.

With only a few days before the 29th she decided to

immediately get to work. She locked herself in her office and listed all of the reasons why her reprimand should be lenient. She then created a speech from this list, and three hours later she left her office feeling good about her chances. She would meet the committee head on.

On the morning of the 29th Julia woke up early and reviewed her argument. She was proud of her accomplishments, and felt that she merited a slap on the wrist at the worst. Julia put on her most conservative suit, fought her way through the reporters who were camped outside her home, and got into her car.

She arrived at the Hartford Town Hall at eight-twenty. She made her way to room 202 and took a seat on a hallway bench. At precisely nine o'clock a man in a dark suit with a stern look on his face invited her to come inside.

The plain room was simply decorated with a single picture, a chair for Julia, and a long table with three very serious looking individuals sitting in judgment. Julia took her seat at the head of the table, and the proceedings began.

"Dr. Pearlman, I'm Dr. Fitzgerald. To my right is Dr. Groothuis, and to my left is Dr. Wenner. We have been asked to determine if a reprimand is appropriate in this case, and if so to what degree that reprimand should entail. Your case has been well chronicled, and so as not to belabor the obvious, this committee would like to hear, in your own words, your defense to some apparently egregious charges."

Julia took a deep breath and took out a prepared speech. "Colleagues," she began, "I met Mr. Victory several years ago while I was doing pro-bono work at his high school. We have continued to work together for the past several years, and while my actions may appear to be reprehensible, especially if you've been reading the papers, I can assure you that Mr. Victory was in an extremely tenuous state when our experiment began, and I honestly felt that my drug was his only viable option. I have always had his best interest in mind, and although things have not worked out well I don't know that I would do anything differently if given a second opportunity without the benefit of hindsight. Furthermore, I have been a doctor in good standing with this state for nearly twenty years without a blemish on my record, and until recently I have been a professor of psychiatry at Yale. I ask this committee to use its discretion to consider the rationale for my actions as well as my previous record, and to please pass a compassionate sentence on my behalf. Thank you."

Julia's heart was racing but she felt good about her speech. It had gone off without a hitch, and Julia truly believed that it had done some good. As she looked at the panel expectantly Dr. Fitzgerald looked to his left and then to his right before addressing Julia.

"Dr. Pearlman, we ask that you wait out in the hallway while the committee discusses this case. We'll call you when we're ready for you," he said in a dismissive fashion.

Julia duly went out into the hall and sat on the bench. She felt as if she was back in grammar school being reprimanded by an angry teacher. Yet she barely had time to catch her breath before Dr. Fitzgerald came back out to fetch her.

"We're ready for you, Doctor."

Julia didn't know if it was a good sign or not that the committee had come to a decision so quickly, but she figured she would find out soon enough. As she took her seat she actually thought that she might be having heart palpitations. Once again Dr. Fitzgerald looked to his left and then to his right as Doctors Groothuis and Wenner both nodded with their endorsement. Dr. Fitzgerald cleared his throat and began.

"Dr. Pearlman, this committee has carefully reviewed all of the evidence, including your record of achievement and volunteer work. However, your actions with Mr. Victory are reprehensible, and there is no excuse for your unethical and frankly quite dangerous behavior. Therefore, this ethics committee, with the powers instilled in us by the state of Connecticut, have unanimously decided to suspend your medical license for a period of two years, to be followed by a five year probationary period, during which time your actions will be closely monitored by a designee of this board. We all hope you fully understand the seriousness of the shall I dare say crime you have committed, and personally Dr. Pearlman, I believe this committee has shown leniency considering the gravity of the incident. That is all."

Julia sat there speechless. As the ethics committee members packed up their belongings Julia was motionless, seemingly frozen in her seat.

"*Two years?*" she said to herself. She could hardly believe it. And then it hit her - maybe her actions were truly as bad as everyone was saying. But two years without practicing medicine? It was her life and her livelihood.

As she pulled herself out of her seat and made her way toward the door she wondered how she would ever recover.

CHAPTER 75

The next two weeks were sheer agony for all involved. Julia was still reeling from the suspension of her medical license. Maria was worried sick about the future of her family. William was completely despondent in prison. Even Mikey, who had seemed to be taking things in stride, was now sensing how ominous the situation was. So when the first day of the trial finally arrived, William, Julia, Maria and Mikey were all, in a strange way, relieved.

That morning Julia and Maria woke up early after another sleepless night. With Mikey still sleeping at six o'clock Julia and Maria sat at Julia's kitchen table, drank coffee, and discussed their game plan.

"Remember what Attorney Herman told us," Julia said to Maria. "Try not to get too agitated during the trial. The district attorney is going to undoubtedly say some nasty things about William, but we have to try and remain calm."

"I will," Maria said, "but I know it's not going to be easy."

"We'll just have to use each other for strength," Julia said as she stretched out her hand and grabbed Maria's across the table. The two women, who came from different worlds, had now actually become good friends. With tears in both of their eyes they knew they would need all of the support they could get.

Two hours later Julia, Maria and Mikey once again fought their way through the mass of reporters outside Julia's house and drove to the courthouse, only to be met by another media blitz there. And if they thought things were bad before they were now in for a rude awakening.

"I can't believe how many there are!" Maria nearly shouted to Julia and Mikey as they pushed their way inside the courthouse doors. Once inside things calmed down, if just a bit. Judge Fisher had hand selected only a specific, small percentage of the media to be allowed into his courtroom to try and keep some semblance of peace. Julia, Maria and Mikey made their way into the reserved seating in the front row, right behind Attorney Herman, as the packed house of spectators gawked at them. Sitting directly across from the threesome, behind the district attorney's table, was the family of the deceased guard. As the grief-stricken group glared at the defense Julia and Maria tired not to make eye contact. With a packed house, it was time for the big entrance.

Attorney Stoler swung open the main doors to the courtroom and grandly walked down the aisle to his table, followed by three assistant district attorneys who tried in vain to keep up. The District Attorney was all business, busily spewing out orders to his cronies when he wasn't scribbling on his own legal pad. The spectators, who were taking in every move, seemed genuinely impressed, and this was not missed by Attorney Stoler. With the tension high enough to be cut by the proverbial knife the heat was about to be turned up a notch. The side door to the courtroom opened up and there he was, the man of the hour, wearing his only suit.

As William Victory made his way to his seat he could literally feel every eyeball in the room glaring at him. Attorney Herman conferred with his client as the courtroom audience sat and waited. After only a few minutes (but what seemed like an eternity), Judge Fisher entered the room. The bailiff called for all to stand but the judge quickly instructed everyone to take their seats with a simple wave of the hand. While some judges would bask in the glow of a high profile case such as this Gorham Fisher couldn't have cared less, and he wasn't about to have his courtroom turned into a circus.

"Ladies and Gentleman, please remember that this is a court of law. I expect everyone to conduct themselves with the utmost of decorum. This is your only warning. If anyone disrupts my courtroom they will be asked to leave, and will not be permitted to return. I trust I have made myself clear." The room quickly grew quiet as all present could immediately tell that the judge meant business.

"Attorney Stoler," Judge Fisher continued. "Please proceed with your opening argument."

Marc Stoler stood up from his seat slowly as if he was in pain. He sighed as he made his way over to the twelve men and women who would ultimately determine William's fate.

"Ladies and Gentlemen of the jury, as you hear the evidence set forth by the state in the coming days and weeks it will become completely self evident that this excuse for a man, William Victory, broke into a secure laboratory at Yale University, killed the guard on duty, stole some very sensitive drugs, and like a coward returned to his apartment only to later hide under the auspices of a bogus insanity defense. We, the state of Connecticut, will unequivocally prove that Mr. Victory not only was of sound mind and body when he committed this heinous crime, but he actually planned out his deadly deed weeks before and confessed his plan to his friend and so called therapist just hours before he acted on it. As this case plays itself out I'm confident that you, the citizens of the great state of Connecticut, will do the only reasonable thing, and the right thing, by coming back with a verdict of guilty of all counts. Thank you."

As the district attorney made his way back to his seat Julia watched the jury members intently. To Julia's dismay she could already tell that several members of the panel already seemed to be nodding in agreement as Attorney Stoler made his opening comments.

"Attorney Herman," Judge Fisher more commanded than stated, "your opening argument."

Brian Herman had been through countless court cases, but as he stood up, similar to the bail hearing several months prior, he actually felt his knees shaking. He steadied himself as he walked as confidently as possible to the jury and made eye contact with each and every member before proceeding. He took a deep breath, looked at his legal pad one more time, and began.

"First of all I will make it perfectly clear that we, the defense in this case, concede that my client, William Victory, did break into the Yale University laboratory, and he did steal some very sensitive drugs. And yes," Brian said, raising his voice, "William even admits to killing the guard on duty." Brian paused as he let his words sink in to the jury. "However, we will prove that William was not of sound mind, and in actuality was clinically and legally insane at the time of the crime. We simply ask that you, as the collective jury, carefully weigh all of the evidence and discipline yourselves to wait until you have heard all of the evidence before making up your mind. Please remember that you are holding a man's life in your hands, and this is not something to throw away lightly. Thank you."

As the whole courtroom watched Attorney Herman only Julia was looking elsewhere. Once again she concentrated on the jury, but this time noticed that several of the members were actually looking at William with disdain. Julia's clinical judgment, and more importantly her gut, told her that things were not starting off well. They were not starting off well at all.

CHAPTER 76

Attorney Stoler spent the day parading around the courtroom like the master of ceremonies at a three ring circus. He began by calling the mother of the deceased, who seemingly began crying before she even sat down in the witness chair. As the District Attorney led her patiently through the examination the jury hung on every word. With the tears flowing she emotionally explained how her son had always been such a good boy. He was her only child, and she had loved him more than life itself. She would only be comforted if she knew that Mr. Victory, 'that cold blooded killer' as she described him, spent the rest of his life behind bars.

After over an hour of questioning there was hardly a dry eye in the courtroom. When Attorney Stoler finally concluded Julia thought that several of the jury members would leap over the railing and try to lynch William on the spot. Judge Fisher then turned the witness over to Attorney Herman. Reasoning that enough damage had been done and hoping to cut his losses, Brian calmly informed the judge that he had no questions for the witness.

Attorney Stoler then called his next witness, the emergency room doctor. The good physician graphically described how the killer had ruthlessly asphyxiated the guard. The doctor surmised that the murderer had been right handed, a male, and approximately six feet tall. These were all characteristics that William possessed, a small fact that was not missed by any of the jury members. When Attorney Stoler finally finished with the doctor Brian only had one question for him.

"Doctor, is there any way that you could predict if the killer was of sound mind at the time of the murder?"

"I couldn't say," answered the witness.

"Thank you," Attorney Herman said quickly before the doctor could elaborate. "No further questions."

Marc Stoler was in all of his glory, and he ended a near perfect day by calling Angelo Campanella to the stand. After several preliminary questions in which Angelo described his position at Yale, affirmatively stated that he was the head of the Psychiatry department and was responsible for overseeing the entire department, the District Attorney didn't waste any time.

"I'll make this brief. Dr. Campanella, did you ever see the defendant on the university campus prior to the alleged crime?"

"Yes I did," Angelo answered unequivocally.

"Would you say you saw him there often?"

"I can remember seeing Mr. Victory in Dr. Pearlman's lab on many occasions."

"Is this the same lab where the drugs in question, the infamous drug that we've all heard so much about, were stolen?"

Angelo glanced at Julia and felt a twinge of remorse, but he had no choice but to be perfectly honest. "Yes, the same one," Angelo answered in a low voice.

"What was that?" Attorney Stoler said almost sarcastically. "I couldn't quite make that out. Could you repeat yourself a little bit louder so we can all hear you clearly?"

"It is the same lab," Angelo said, a little bit louder this time.

"Thank you, Doctor."

And with that Judge Fisher mercifully pronounced that the court would recess for the day. Brian, Julia, Maria, Mikey, and most importantly William all went to their respective residences to lick their wounds and pray that things would get better. They simply couldn't get any worse.

CHAPTER 77

Since the murder the amount of press coverage had appeared to be at full force. Yet now that the trial was underway Julia and Maria couldn't help but long for the days when the reporters simply followed their every step in public. Now the press was literally peeking into the windows of Julia's house. The invasion of privacy appeared to be unprecedented, but there was nothing to do but say 'no comment,' try to keep their cool, and pray that one day a sense of normalcy would be regained. However, that day did not appear to be anywhere in the near future.

After another morning of fighting off reporters Julia, Maria and Mikey made their way into the sanctuary of the courtroom. Unfortunately, for the next several days the threesome would have to listen to the District Attorney call therapist after therapist and psychiatrist after psychiatrist to the stand to testify to William's sanity. Without reservation, each so called 'expert' vehemently testified that the likelihood of William undergoing a dissociative state was virtually impossible.

"It's a very, very rare condition. Mr. Victory wasn't under nearly enough stress to trigger such a state. He was of sound mind and body at the time of the crime."

And on and on it went. Attorney Herman fought valiantly to discredit each and every witness but it was obvious to all, especially Julia, that the jury was buying the expert testimony hook, line and sinker. By the time the District Attorney had finished with the multitude of 'experts' three more days had passed, and by the time Attorney Stoler was finished grand standing another week had come and gone. When the prosecution finally rested irrevocable damage had already been done.

Brian Herman had enough legal experience to realize that the last thing the tired jury wanted was to sit through another week of long, drawn out testimony. If his client had any chance at all he would have to be short, precise, and most importantly damn convincing. Judge Fisher began week three of the trial by announcing that the defense could now call its first witness. Brian stood up, cleared his throat, and called Dr. Julia Pearlman to the stand.

Julia walked confidently to the witness stand but the hatred in the room was almost palpable. Brian began by having Julia list her credentials, and even the now-biased jury had to admit they were impressive. Brian had instructed Julia that the only plausible plan of action was to be totally forthcoming. For one she was under oath, and secondly, and more importantly, the truth would come out eventually - the District Attorney would see to that.

As Brian adeptly led the examination Julia detailed her entire relationship with William. She began when they met at William's high school and clearly and coherently spoke of his learning disability, low self esteem, trial with the drug and its subsequent side effects, and ended with his fight with Maria that led to the dissociative state and murder of the guard. Julia was poised, professional and convincing, and even a veteran like Brian was impressed with how well she had preformed. After nearly a day's worth of testimony Brian sensed that perhaps the tide was beginning to turn.

"I have no further questions for Dr. Pearlman," Brian informed the judge and began to return to his table. But before he could even sit down and catch his breath Attorney Stoler had leapt to his feet like a lion that had just been freed from his cage.

"Your witness counselor," Judge Fisher stated. As the District Attorney strutted in front of Julia and the jury a smirk crossed his smug face.

"Dr. Pearlman," he said, sarcasm streaming from his voice, "and I use the term doctor lightly. Isn't it true that your license to practice medicine has been suspended?"

"Yes," Julia said matter -of-factly, "it has."

"And isn't it also true that you illegally administered a drug that was not FDA approved to Mr. Victory which eventually led to a psychotic episode?"

"Yes, but that was only because…" But Attorney Stoler cut her off.

"And isn't it also true that you care for the defendant deeply and would do anything in your power to help him in any way possible?"

"I wouldn't lie for him if that's what you're implying," Julia said indignantly.

"That's exactly what I'm implying!" the District Attorney nearly shouted. "I submit that you are an unethical doctor who has a perverse relationship with a murderer. I further submit that you are now lying to this courtroom in an attempt to free a clearly guilty man."

At this Brian had had enough and jumped to his feet. "Is there a question forthcoming?" he asked loudly.

"I'm done with this so-called expert," the District Attorney said with as much disdain as he could muster. And with that Julia's previous testimony was all but forgotten. She sulked out of the witness chair and took her seat.

Thankfully Julia was the only witness of the day. Brian knew that things were desperate. He asked Julia, Maria and Mikey to meet him at the jail to have a pow-wow with William. A half an hour later the five members of the team were assembled in the jail's conference room, and it was obvious to all that things were not going well. Brian sat quietly for a moment in a pensive state before speaking. After several minutes of silence he began with what everyone was thinking.

"These are dire times. It's clear to me that the jury is against us, and we need to take a bold stand in order to turn the tide. I'm proposing that we put William on the stand, but I want to make sure that we're all in agreement before we do so. I'm open to any comments or suggestions." William, Maria and Mikey, per usual, looked to Julia to take the lead.

"Brian," Julia began, "haven't you said from the beginning that you felt William should invoke his fifth amendment right and refuse to testify? I thought you felt that the District Attorney would crucify him on cross examination."

"You're right, Julia," Brian responded, "but we're desperate. If we don't take a huge chance I can tell you with the utmost of confidence that William is doomed. I think the jury wants to hear William testify, and I believe only a perfect performance by William will potentially turn the jury."

William, who was never a big talker, had been unusually quiet even for him throughout the entire trial process. But with his life literally on the line he felt compelled to speak. "I'll do it," he nearly whispered. "I've got nothing to lose. Even an idiot like me can tell I'm in big trouble. Like Brian said, I'm doomed if I don't testify, and things can't get any worse than they already are." William then turned his attention to Brian. "Yeah, I'll do it," he said with as much conviction as he could summon.

"Are we all in agreement?" Brian said to the group. Julia looked at Maria and Mikey, then spoke for everyone.

"I believe we are."

"Good," said Brian.

Julia, Maria and Mikey said their goodbyes and left Brian and William, who would be discussing strategy until the wee hours of the morning. It was now or never.

CHAPTER 78

The next morning Brian entered the courtroom bleary-eyed with a large cup of coffee in hand. He had virtually been up for the entire night working. But despite his fatigue he felt energized, and his adrenaline was pumping. As the room filled once again to capacity Judge Fisher called his court to order.

"Does the defense have any further witnesses?"

"Yes, your honor. The defense calls William Victory to the stand." An audible gasp was let out by the collective onlookers as Judge Fisher rapped his gavel.

"Order in the court," he commanded.

William was pale and shaken as he forced himself to stand up and walk to the witness stand. As the bailiff swore him in his mind was swimming, and he could barely comprehend what was transpiring before him. When the bailiff finished he managed to squeak out an, "I do."

Brian could sense how uncomfortable William was and

mouthed the words 'take a deep breath' before he began. William inhaled deeply, then Brian started off with the easiest questions he could think of in an attempt to put his client at ease.

"Please state your full name."

"William Nathan Victory," he answered with a shaky voice.

"Where were you born?"

"Right here in Connecticut," William said with slightly more confidence.

After several more perfunctory questions Brian got to the meat of the matter. "Now William, in your own words can you please explain to the good people of the jury exactly what happened?"

William knew this question was coming. He and Brian had spent half the night discussing exactly how he would answer it. Yet when the time actually came he froze. He couldn't remember anything that they had discussed. As all eyes were on him an interminable five seconds passed in silence. And then another ten seconds. Brian tried to break the tension.

"William, I know you're nervous. Please just try and remember everything you can about the night of the break in and murder." William took another deep breath and thankfully began talking. Unfortunately, he was so nervous and sleep deprived that his mind was almost completely dysfunctional. The result was a rambling speech that one would need a map to follow, and in the end made no sense at all. Brian did his best to redirect William often but to no avail. William had bombed on the stand, and after forty-five minutes of futility Brian had all but given up, but gave one last ditch effort to put a good spin on things.

"Thank you William. I know that was hard for you, but we all appreciate you doing your best in recapping what was obviously a painful memory." As Brian walked back to his table he had déjà vu as he watched the District Attorney once again jump out of his seat, this time apparently licking his chops.

"Mr. Victory," the D.A. began, "do you really expect the good people of New Haven to believe that bizarre tale? To be perfectly honest I couldn't even follow half of what you were saying." As Attorney Stoler walked toward the jury he continued. "Isn't it true, Mr. Victory, that your story is so full of holes and lies that you can't even follow it yourself?"

"No," William sputtered. "It's just that I'm nervous, and because of my learning disability it makes it hard for me to think clearly."

"So now you can't think clearly, but you sure appeared to be thinking clearly when you killed an innocent man and stole some very sensitive drugs from a secured lab, just like you admitted telling your so-called therapist before you committed this cowardly crime. Isn't that right?"

"I didn't mean to do those things. I can't even remember doing them."

The District Attorney could sense blood and was going in for the kill. "Mr. Victory, I only have one more question. Do you really expect this courtroom to believe that by your own admission you were in a desperate state? By your own admission you would have done anything in your power to change your lot in life. By your own admission you confessed your plan to Dr. Pearlman ahead of time. By your own admission you wanted those drugs more than life itself. By your own admission you admit to killing the guard and robbing the lab, even though you contest you don't remember doing so. And you expect this courtroom to believe that you didn't mean to do it because of some bogus dissociative state?" The D.A. was now railing to whoever would listen. "Is that what you contest, Mr. Victory!?" Attorney Stoler was so convincing that even William wasn't sure what he believed anymore. As he sat dumbfounded the courtroom waited for him to answer. "Well Mr. Victory?" the D.A. snarled. "We're waiting."

The only thing that came out of William's mouth was a pathetic, "I'm not sure."

"You're not sure? Well I'll tell you what I'm sure of - that you're a cowardly killer. I'm as sure of that as the day is long."

"Objection," Brian stated, jumping to his feet.

"Withdrawn. I have no further questions for this witness," the District Attorney said with as much disdain as he could muster.

As the courtroom buzzed the Judge once again rapped his gavel. "If you have no further witnesses, Attorney Herman, we'll move on to closing arguments." Brian simply put up his hands to indicate he was through. "Attorney Stoler, your closing arguments please."

The D.A. had barely gotten into his seat before he was back up, pacing in front of the jury.

"Ladies and Gentleman of the great state of Connecticut, in my twenty-seven years of practicing law I have rarely seen a case that was as open and shut as the one in front of you today. You have been witness to a case in which this cowardly defendant has stolen some very sensitive drugs and committed a horrific murder. Mr. Victory has admitted to these acts, and is now hiding behind a bogus temporary insanity defense. You have heard expert after expert testify that this so called dissociative state is a very rare condition. A condition so rare that the odds that the defendant actually experienced it are slim to none, with an emphasis on none. And the only argument the defense put forth was a discredited therapist and a defendant who couldn't even keep his own bogus alibi straight. Ladies and Gentleman, this is obviously a high profile case. The country and the world are watching, and you have a huge responsibility. Please do the right thing. I implore you. The only reasonable thing a rationale jury could possible conclude - a verdict of guilty on all counts. Thank you."

Attorney Stoler was basking in the moment. As he strutted back to his table he could hardly contain a smile. This one was money in the bank, and a shot at the governorship couldn't be far behind.

Brian knew things were desperate. If his client had any chance at all he was going to have to give the best closing argument of his career. He stood up, walked slowly to the jury, and once again looked each member straight in the eyes before beginning.

"Distinguished members of the jury," he began, "you have an awesome responsibility in front of you, for you hold a man's life in your hands. My client, William Victory, is a legally innocent man. Despite what the District Attorney would like you to believe, William was legally insane at the time of the robbery and murder. He is a good person, just like the twelve members of this jury. Unfortunately William has had to suffer with a severe learning disability that has devastated him for his entire life. And after struggling with tremendous stress, he finally snapped. A dissociative state is a psychologically documented disorder. Is it a rare disorder? Yes, I concede that it is. However, does it strike unsuspecting victims no matter how rarely? Yes it does. And did William suffer from just such an episode? I submit that he did, and subsequently committed the robbery and murder while at the mercy of the aforementioned dissociative state. Now ladies and gentleman, what I'm going to say now is extremely important, so please give me your attention for just thirty more seconds. You may not believe my client. You may feel that this entire defense of a dissociative state is completely bogus. But if there is any doubt in your mind as to whether or not William was legally insane at the time of the crime, you most likely have reasonable doubt. And with reasonable doubt you must come back with a verdict of not guilty. Please ladies and gentlemen, please think long and hard before determining that this legally insane man is guilty. For his life depends on it. Thank you."

Brian stood in front of the jury for just an extra instant before returning to his seat. He wanted to try and get a quick glance at the reaction of the jury members. Unfortunately, when he did Brian didn't like what he saw. Several of the jury members were shaking their heads from side to side and several others were frowning. As Brian returned to his seat he prayed that he had gotten through to at least one of the jury. If just one member could hold out against the pressure of what seemed to be a vengeful jury maybe, just maybe, he or she could hang the jury and they would live to fight another day. But a seasoned veteran like Attorney Herman had to concede that it didn't look good. It didn't look good at all.

CHAPTER 79

With the jury conferring over William's fate Brian, Julia, Maria, Mikey, and most importantly William all sat around a metal table in a cramped courthouse room with two guards standing outside the only exit. There wasn't much left to do but worry and wait. Brian was honest and told the group that their best bet was to hope for a hung jury. He also let them know that the longer the jury deliberated the better William's chances were. For if the jury deliberated for many hours, or better yet several days, it probably meant that they were having difficulty agreeing on a decision. And without a unanimous vote the jury would be hung. The five friends simply sat silently staring at the clock and praying.

But after only forty-five minutes a guard was knocking on the door. A verdict had been rendered. Julia, Maria and Mikey all looked to Brian, who said nothing. It was William who suddenly and uncharacteristically took charge. He stood up, and all eyes were on him.

"I just want you all to know that I appreciate everything. No matter what happens I want you all to know how much you mean to me. I ain't got much, but I do know that you guys are all my family. No matter what happens…" As William's voice trailed off Brian, Maria and Mikey stood up as well, but Julia remained in her seat. She had that ever-present pit in her stomach and just knew that things were going to end in disaster.

With all of the respective members back in the courthouse Judge Fisher addressed the jury. "Have you reached a decision?"

The foreman spoke. "We have, your honor."

"Then what say you?"

"We find the defendant, William Victory, guilty on all counts."

The courthouse let out a gasp and a few members of the guard's family hugged. Judge Fisher banged his gavel.

"Ladies and Gentlemen of the jury, the court thanks you for your assistance. You are free to go. Bailiff, take Mr. Victory into custody. This courtroom is adjourned."

As a stoic William was being led away Maria sobbed loudly and fell into Julia's arms, and Mikey looked to Julia for an explanation.

"When does William get to come home, Julie?"

"I'm not sure," Julia answered. "The judge will tell us at the sentencing hearing." But Julia knew all too well that William would never be coming home again.

CHAPTER 80

After several painstaking weeks the group reassembled at the courthouse to hear William's sentence. With Julia, Maria and Mikey once again sitting in the front row, the cloud over their heads was almost palpable. Brian sat right in front of them with his hands folded. There was nothing left to do at this point but wait.

With the courtroom thirsty for blood William entered the room through a side door with his feet in shackles, wearing an orange jumpsuit and with a guard on each arm. The ever-present Judge Fisher was, per usual, all business, but on this day he seemed to be in an ornery mood as well as he addressed Brian.

"Mr. Herman, does your client have anything he would like to say before sentencing takes place?"

"Yes, your honor. Mr. Victory would like to make a statement."

Brian and William had spent the previous night working out the details of the speech that William was to read. But when William stood with his hands shaking he put the letter down, looked at the deceased guard's family, and simply uttered, "I'm real sorry." He then quickly sat back in his seat, completely despondent and defeated.

"Is that all you have to say Mr. Victory?" Judge Fisher more scolded than asked. William could only nod his head up and down. "Mr. Victory," the judge began, "in all my years on the bench, that was one of the most pathetic attempts at reconciliation I've ever witnessed. It is clear to me, and I believe to all of the citizens of New Haven, that you have lied, stolen and killed, and yet you don't seem to be the least bit remorseful. It sickens me to see a good for nothing murderer like yourself sit here smugly while a family grieves just several feet away from you. You leave me no choice but to sentence you to lifetime imprisonment at the Hartford Maximum Security Penitentiary with no option for parole. Guards, get this disgrace of a man out of my sight."

As the bailiff grabbed William's arm a little more tightly than was necessary William simply looked at the floor, but Maria's sobbing was more than audible. As the members of the courtroom began to gather their belongings the unthinkable occurred. Suddenly, in one swift movement William grabbed the bailiff in a choke hold and ripped his gun from his holster.

"Get back, get back!" a crazed William screamed as he pointed the gun at the unsuspecting bailiff's head. In what seemed like a split second several guards had their guns aimed at William as most of the courtroom viewers hit the floor.

"I can't spend the rest of my life in that hell hole!" William shouted for all to hear. As the guards began to close in on William he backed himself up to the wall while continuing to hold the petrified guard as a shield, the black pistol pointed directly at his head. "Don't come any closer," William warned. "I'll kill this cop! I swear I will!"

And no one in the room doubted him. With Judge Fisher and most of the courtroom frozen with fear for a moment no one moved. With the moment at its most perilous Julia stood and slowly walked toward William.

"Dr. Pearlman, don't come any closer or this man's a goner."

Julia stopped dead in her tracks, and although her heart was racing she kept a calm demeanor. "William," she said softly, "I'm begging you. Think about what you're doing. I know things look incredibly bleak right now, but I promise you this is not the correct path. You're better than this, William. You've got a wife and son to think about. Please William, don't do this."

William just stood motionless, tears streaming down his face. "I'm sorry Dr. Pearlman. I'm sorry I dragged you down with my pathetic life." Then William turned and faced Maria, who was as white as a ghost. "Babe, you gotta know that I love you and only wanted to do right by you. Always tell Itzy that his father loved him," he whispered. Instantly Julia knew what was about to occur.

"William, don't do it!" she screamed, but it was too late.

William shoved the terrified guard to the floor, stuck the gun deep into his mouth and pulled the trigger. The bang resonated throughout the halls of the courthouse. William lay motionless on the floor, blood spilling from his gruesome, suddenly disfigured head. Most of the onlookers couldn't bear to witness the hideous scene, but Julia rushed to his side. While medically Julia knew there was nothing left to do she instinctively ran to William and knelt beside him, holding his bloody body next to hers. William was dead, and there was nothing Julia, Maria or anyone could do. William was gone.

CHAPTER 81

As devastating as the day's events were, what was to follow was nearly as traumatic. Julia accompanied Maria to the morgue, and the press became so intrusive that the two women were actually given a police escort just to get around the city. Julia did her best to stay strong, but she felt like jelly on the inside. Maria was simply a complete wreck from the inside out. She couldn't stop crying, she threw up several times, and for the most part she couldn't even answer simple questions. With Julia's medical license suspended she called on a colleague to prescribe some tranquilizers for Maria.

At the end of the longest day Julia, Maria and Mikey had ever experienced they finally made their way to the daycare to pick up Itzy. Itzy's babysitter, like the rest of the country, had heard about the day's events and agreed to stay late. When the group finally made their way through the reporters and back to Julia's house they were literally exhausted. Julia helped put Itzy in his crib and got Maria ready for bed. Maria took two of the tranquilizers and lay down.

"I'll be right in the next room," Julia told Maria. "If you need anything at all, even if it seems minute, don't hesitate to knock on my door."

"Thanks Dr. Pearlman. I appreciate all you've done for us," Maria whimpered. "William considered you like family, and so do I. You'll never truly know how much you meant to us."

Julia had never seen Maria quite so emotional but obviously chalked it up to the day's horrifying events. "You are my family, Maria. Now try and get some sleep." As Julia was exiting the room she faintly heard Maria whisper, "I love you."

Julia mechanically brushed her teeth, washed her face, put her pajamas on and got into bed. Her mind was racing. *How could this have happened?* She began to blame herself. *How could I have been so stupid?* she wondered. *How could I have administered the drug to William before it was FDA approved? If only I had been more responsible and acted like a professional. I broke the cardinal rule and let myself get emotionally involved, and now look what happened. It's all my fault.* As the reality of this insight began to unfold Julia felt the tears streaming down her face. She lay in bed crying for nearly two hours before she finally fell asleep in utter exhaustion.

CHAPTER 82

The next morning Julia awoke late. It was almost ten o'clock as she forced herself to get up and face what was sure to be another excruciating day. She entered the living room and found Mikey watching cartoons. As she began to clear the cobwebs from her mind she locked in on a wailing sound. At first she thought it was coming from outside, but she suddenly realized that it was Itzy crying from inside Maria's bedroom.

Julia walked to the door and knocked but there was no answer. She knocked again, a little louder, with no response but the tearful cries coming from Itzy. She knocked one more time even louder, and this time the force of the blow pushed the door open. She peered inside to see Itzy standing up in his crib, hysterical, but Maria was passed out cold.

Julia approached the side of the bed and gently shook Maria's shoulder, but Maria didn't respond. *Wow,* Julia thought, *she's really passed out.* Julia shook Maria again with no response. And then, out of the corner of her eye, Julia saw it lying on the floor - the bottle of tranquilizers. She snatched it up, and to her dismay it was empty.

"Oh my God!" she screamed. She immediately grabbed Maria's wrist and thought she felt a faint pulse, but she couldn't be sure. She sprinted to the kitchen and called 911. Minutes later an ambulance was at her house, and when the paramedics came through the door the press photographers veraciously snapped pictures.

Julia grabbed Itzy, and moments later Maria was being rushed away down the street toward Mercy Memorial Hospital with Julia, Itzy and Mikey in tow. Julia held Itzy in her arms as the paramedics attended to Maria. Thankfully there wasn't much traffic at this time of day and they made it to the hospital without delay. As they pulled up to the emergency room Maria was whisked away as Julia, Itzy and Mikey were led to the waiting room. After only thirty minutes a doctor appeared grim faced. Julia knew that look all too well and braced herself as she stood to hear the grave details.

"I'm terribly sorry," the doctor began. "There was nothing we could do. Mrs. Victory was pronounced dead on arrival. I'm so sorry."

At first Julia couldn't believe what she was hearing, but as she looked down into Itzy's unsuspecting eyes the reality of the situation hit her. First she became light–headed, and then the room began to spin. Julia had the sense to hand Itzy to the doctor before everything went black.

The next thing Julia knew she woke up in a hospital bed with a sympathetic nurse looking over her. "What happened?" Julia asked as she looked around the room.

"You fainted, Dr. Pearlman," the nurse responded with extra care in her voice. "Here, why don't you try and drink a little orange juice and the doctor will be in to check on you in a minute."

Julia took a couple of sips from her cup and began to feel better. But the reality of Maria's death quickly overwhelmed her once again, and she just had to get out of there. She didn't know where she would go or who to turn to for help, but she just knew she had to leave. With nowhere else to turn Julia made the only call she could.

About forty-five minutes later Angelo Campanella came rushing in to Julia's hospital room, his face a mask of concern. "Oh my God, Julia. I came as quickly as I could. I'm so sorry. What can I do?"

"I know your kids are all grown up Ang, but would you mind looking after a one-year-old and my brother Mikey for a couple of hours?"

"Not a problem, Julia. I'd be happy to."

"One of the nurses is looking after them for the time being. I'll have her release them to you. Thank you, Angelo," she said, tears welling up in her eyes once again."

"You're welcome. Take all the time you need."

With no destination in mind Julia got in a taxi and told the driver to simply drive around for a while. After about a half an hour she realized that the meter was starting to get a little high and instructed the driver to take her home. It was the last place she wanted to be but there were really no other alternatives. She fought through the press once again which had lessened, if just a little, now that the trial was over, and took off her coat. As she looked around her old Victorian it seemed so cold and empty. She thought about getting into bed and hiding under the covers for a while, but something was drawing her back to Maria's room. As she pushed open the door an eerie feeling encapsulated the room. She walked in and looked around. And there, sitting prevalently on the nightstand, was a piece of paper folded in two. She wondered how she missed it before. With her hands shaking she gingerly picked up the note and began reading.

Dear Dr. Pearlman,

I know I'm not thinking rationally, and I know that if I discussed this with you that you would try and talk me out of this, but I just can't go on without William. I know that from deep inside my heart. My only reason for living is for Itzy, but I could never be a good mother to him. Not now. Not without William. I know William would support my decision to have you raise him. Will and I both knew that you always wanted children of your own but never got the chance, and it's obvious how much you love Itzy and how much he loves you. Please, Dr. Pearlman, never let Itzy forget his parents, and always remind him how much we loved him.

Yours always, Maria.

Julia read the letter again. And then for a third time. She couldn't believe that both William and Maria were gone. But they were. She lay down on the floor and curled up into a ball. *How had things gone so wrong?* she asked herself for the hundredth time. How had things gone so very wrong?

CHAPTER 83

Angelo dropped Mikey and Itzy off later that night, and two days later the combined funeral for William and Maria took place. Due to the embarrassment surrounding the murder and subsequent trial the Victory's had basically been disowned by their family and the few friends that they had. Consequently, the funeral was sparsely attended. Julia held Itzy in her arms and sat next to Mikey. Besides a couple of distant relatives on Maria's side, the church was empty. Julia couldn't even summon up the strength to prepare a eulogy. Father Mulcahey said a few polite words, and after a quick graveside service it was over. William and Maria were buried side by side for eternity. Two lives gone too soon with so much left to give. But alas, it was not to be.

Later that evening, Julia and Mikey sat on the sofa as Julia rocked Itzy back and forth in an effort to get him to stop crying. Mikey turned to his sister with a look of confusion on his face.

"Why is the baby crying, Julie?"

"I think he misses his mommy and daddy," Julia responded, her heart breaking. Another moment passed. Mikey turned to Julia once again, looking remorseful.

"I'm sorry, Julie. I didn't mean for this to happen."

"For what to happen, Mikey?"

"I was just trying to help William be smart."

"What are you talking about, Mikey?"

Mikey took a deep breath. "I know I'm not supposed to, but I was listening at the door when William told you how he wanted to tie up the guard and steal the drugs. I figured if I did it William wouldn't get in trouble, so I did everything he said. I broke in just like he said. But I didn't mean to kill the guard. I guess I just tied the gag too tight around his mouth. So then I took the drugs and put them in William's apartment after work and then I came home. I figured he would take the drugs and be smart again and everyone would be happy."

Julia was speechless. "What are you saying, Mikey? How could you have done this?!" she nearly screamed.

"Willie was my friend, and you're supposed to try and help your friends, right Julie?"

Julia was dumbfounded. She sat there completely numb until Itzy's wailing brought her back to the present.

"I'm really sorry Julie," Mikey said. "I'm not going to get into any trouble, am I?" he asked with the innocent eyes of a child.

"I'm not sure, Mikey," Julia answered somberly. And then, as Julia sat there on the sofa rocking Itzy back and forth, it hit her. She had made a vow for her whole life that she would do everything in her power to protect her brother. It was a vow she made every day of her life.

But now she had the biggest decision of her life in front of her. She could stand by her vow and keep Mikey's secret, or she could vindicate her dear friends, William and Maria, by telling the world the truth. As Itzy continued to cry Julia knew that it was a lose-lose situation. Either decision would devastate Julia for the rest of her life. What seemed like a bad dream had turned into a full-blown nightmare, and Julia knew that, once again, this was only the beginning.

-The End-